C.G.D Roberts

The Forge in the Forest

C.G.D Roberts

The Forge in the Forest

ISBN/EAN: 9783337341435

Printed in Europe, USA, Canada, Australia, Japan

Cover: Foto ©Andreas Hilbeck / pixelio.de

More available books at **www.hansebooks.com**

Being
*The Narrative of the Acadian Ranger, Jean
de Mer, Seigneur de Briart; and how
he crossed the Black Abbé; and of
his Adventures in a Strange
Fellowship*

By

Charles G. D. Roberts

Author of " The Kindred of the Wild," " Barbara
Ladd," " A Sister to Evangeline," etc.

New York
Grosset & Dunlap
Publishers

To

George E. Fenety, Esq.

This Story of a Province
among whose Honoured Sons he is
not least distinguished
is dedicated
with esteem and affection

Contents

Part I. — Marc

Page

A Foreword 11

Chapter

I. The Capture at the Forge . . 15

II. The Black Abbé 27

III. Tamin's Little Stratagem . . . 33

IV. The Governor's Signature . . 46

V. In the Run of the Seas . . . 60

VI. Grûl 72

VII. The Commander is Embarrassed . 85

VIII. The Black Abbé Comes to Dinner . 98

IX. The Abbé Strikes Again . . . 111

X. A Bit of White Petticoat . . . 124

XI. I Fall a Willing Captive . . . 137

Part II. — Mizpah

XII. In a Strange Fellowship . . . 155

XIII. My Comrade 167

XIV. My Comrade Shoots Excellently Well 178

XV. Grûl's Hour 193

Contents

Chapter		Page
XVI.	I Cool My Adversaries' Courage	207
XVII.	A Night in the Deep	219
XVIII.	The Osprey, of Plymouth	229
XIX.	The Camp by Canseau Strait	242
XX.	The Fellowship Dissolved	257
XXI.	The Fight at Grand Pré	272
XXII.	The Black Abbé Strikes in the Dark	287
XXIII.	The Rendezvous at the Forge	302

LIST OF ILLUSTRATIONS

PAGE

"On a block just inside the door sat Marc" (*See page 15*) . . *Frontispiece*

"His head drooped forward upon his breast" 43

"The result of the shot was all that we could desire" 65

"The visitor . . . was none other than the Black Abbé himself . . . 100

"'But I am strong, truly'" . . . 168

"Swinging over the deep, with shudderings and twistings" . . . 200

"And suddenly . . . put Philip into my arms" 310

Part I

Marc

The Forge in the Forest

A Foreword

WHERE the Five Rivers flow down to meet the swinging of the Minas tides, and the Great Cape of Blomidon bars out the storm and the fog, lies half a county of rich meadow-lands and long-arcaded orchards. It is a deep-bosomed land, a land of fat cattle, of well-filled barns, of ample cheeses and strong cider; and a well-conditioned folk inhabit it. But behind this countenance of gladness and peace broods the memory of a vanished people. These massive dykes, whereon twice daily the huge tide beats in vain, were built by hands not suffered to possess the fruits of their labour. These comfortable fields have been scorched with the ruin of burning homes, drenched with the tears of women hurried into exile. These orchard lanes, appropriate to the laughter of children or the silences of lovers, have rung with battle and run deep with blood. Though the race whose bane he was has gone, still stalks the sinister shadow of the Black Abbé.

The low ridge running between the dykelands of the Habitants and the dykelands of the Canard still carries patches of forest interspersed among its farms, for its soil is sandy and not greatly to be coveted for tillage. These patches are but meagre second growth, with here and there a gnarled birch or overpeering pine, lonely survivor of the primeval brotherhood. The undergrowth has long smoothed out all traces of what a curious eye might fifty years ago have discerned, — the foundations of the chimney of a blacksmith's forge. It is a mould well steeped in fateful devisings, this which lies forgotten under the creeping roots of juniper and ragged-robin, between the diminished stream of Canard and the yellow tide of Habitants.

The forest then was a wide-spreading solemnity of shade wherein armies might have moved unseen. The forge stood where the trail from Pereau ran into the more travelled road from the Canard to Grand Pré. The branches of the ancient wood came down all about its low eaves; and the squirrels and blue jays chattered on its roof. It was a place for the gathering of restless spirits, the men of Acadie who hated to accept the flag of the English king. It was the Acadian headquarters of the noted ranger, Jean de Mer, who was still called by courtesy, and by the grace of such of his people as adhered to his altered fortunes, the Seigneur de Briart. His father had been lord of the whole region between Blomidon and Grand Pré; but the English occupation had deprived him of all open and formal lordship, for the de Briart sword was notably conspicuous on the side of New France. Nevertheless, many of Jean de Mer's habitants maintained to him a chivalrous allegiance, and paid him rents for lands which in the English eye were freehold properties. He cherished his hold upon these faithful folk, willing by all honest means to keep their hearts to France. His one son, Marc, grew up at Grand Pré, save for the three years of his studying at Quebec. His faithful retainer, Babin, wielding a smith's hammer at the Forge, had ears of wisdom and a tongue of discretion for the men who came and went. Once or twice in the year, it was de Mer's custom to visit the Grand Pré country, where he would set his hand to the work of the forge after Babin's fashion, playing his part to the befooling of English eyes, and taking, in truth, a quaint pride in his pretended craft. At the time, however, when this narrative opens, he had been a whole three years absent from the Acadian land, and his home-coming was yet but three days old.

Chapter I

The Capture at the Forge

IT was good to be alive that afternoon. A speckled patch of sunshine, having pushed its way through the branches across the road, lay spread out on the dusty floor of the forge. On a block just inside the door sat Marc, his lean, dark face, — the Belleisle face, made more hawklike by the blood of his Penobscot grandmother, — all aglow with eagerness. The lazy youngster was not shamed at the sight of my diligence, but talked right on, with a volubility which would have much displeased his Penobscot grandmother. It was pleasant to be back with the lad again, and I was aweary of the war, which of late had kept my feet forever on the move from Louisbourg to the Richelieu. My fire gave a cheerful roar as I heaved upon the bellows, and turned my pike-point in the glowing charcoal. As the roar sighed down into silence there was a merry whirr of wings, and a covey of young partridges flashed across the road. A contented mind and a full stomach do often make a man a fool, or I should have made shift to inquire why the partridges had so sharply taken wing. But I never thought of it. I turned, and let the iron grow cool, and leaned with one foot on the anvil, to hear the boy's talk. My soul was indeed asleep, lulled by content, or I would surely have felt the gleam of the beady eyes that watched me through a chink in the logs beside the chimney. But I felt those eyes no more than if I had been a log myself.

"Yes, Father," said Marc, pausing in rich contemplation of the picture in his mind's eye, "you would like her hair ! It is unmistakably red, — a chestnut red. But her sister's is redder still !"

I smiled at his knowledge of my little weakness for hair of that colour ; but not of a woman's hair was I thinking at that moment, or I should surely have made some question about the sister. My mind ran off upon another trail.

"And what do the English think they're going to do when de Ramezay comes down upon them?" I inquired. "Do they flatter themselves their tumble-down Annapolis is strong enough to hold us off?"

The lad flushed resentfully and straightened himself up on his seat.

"Do you suppose, Father, that I was in the fort, and hobnobbing with the Governor?" he asked coldly. "I spoke with none of the English save Prudence and her sister, and the child."

"But why not?" said I, unwilling to acknowledge that I had said anything at which he might take offence. "Every one knows your good disposition toward the English, and I should suppose you were in favour at Annapolis. The Governor, I know, makes much of all our people who favour the English cause."

Marc stood up, — lean, and fine, and a good half head taller than his father, —

and looked at me with eyes of puzzled wrath.

"And you think that I, knowing all I do of de Ramezay's plans, would talk to the English about them!" he exclaimed in a voice of keen reproach.

Now, I understood his anger well enough, and in my heart rejoiced at it; for though I knew his honour would endure no stain, I had nevertheless feared lest I should find his sympathies all English. He was a lad with a way of thinking much and thinking for himself, and even now, at twenty year, far more of a scholar than I had ever found time to be. Therefore, I say, his indignation pleased me mightily. Nevertheless I kept at him.

"Chut!" said I, "all the world knows by now of de Ramezay's plans. There had been no taint of treachery in talking of them!"

Marc sat down again, and the ghost of a smile flickered over his lean face. Though free enough of his speech betimes, he was for the most part as unsmiling as an Indian.

"I see you are mocking me, Father," he said presently, relighting his pipe. "Indeed, you know very well I am on your side, for weal or ill. As long as there was a chance of the English being left in peaceable possession of Acadie, I urged that we should accept their rule fully and in good faith. No one can say they haven't ruled us gently and generously. And I feel right sure they will continue to rule us, for the odds are on their side in the game they play with France. But seeing that the game has yet to be played out, there is only one side for me, and I believe it to be the losing one. Though as a boy I liked them well enough, I have nothing more to do with the English now except to fight them. How could I have another flag than yours?"

"You are my own true lad, whatever our difference of opinion!" said I. And if my voice trembled in a manner that might show a softness unsuited to a veteran of my training, bear in mind that, till within the past three days, I had not

seen the lad for three years, and then but
briefly.   At Grand Pré, and in Quebec at
school, Marc had grown up outside my
roving life, and I was just opening my
eyes to find a comrade in this tall son
of my boyhood's love.   His mother, a
daughter of old Baron St. Castin by his
Penobscot wife, had died while he was yet
at the breast.   A babe plays but a small
part in the life of a ranging bush-fighter,
though I had ever a great tenderness for
the little lad.   Now, however, I was looking upon him with new eyes.

Having blown the coals again into a
heat, I returned to Marc's words, certain
of which had somewhat stuck in my
crop.

" But you speak with despondence, lad,
of the chances of the war, and of the hope
of Acadie !   By St. Joseph, we'll drive the
English all the way back of the Penobscot
before you're a twelvemonth older.   And
Acadie will see the Flag of the Lilies flapping once more over the ramparts of Port
Royal."

Marc shook his head slowly, and seemed

to be following with his eyes the vague pattern of the shadows on the floor.

"It seems to me," said he, with a conviction which caught sharply at my heart even though I bore in mind his youth and inexperience, "that rather will the Flag of the Lilies be cast down even from the strong walls of Quebec. But may that day be far off! As for our people here in Acadie, during the last twelvemonth it has been made very clear to me that evil days are ahead. The Black Abbé is preparing many sorrows for us here in Acadie."

"I suppose you mean La Garne!" said I. "He's a diligent servant to France; but I hate a bad priest. He's a dangerous man to cross, Marc! Don't go out of your way to make an enemy of the Black Abbé!"

Again that ghost of a smile glimmered on Marc's lips.

"I fear you speak too late, Father!" said he, quietly. "The reverend Abbé has already marked me. He so far honours me as to think that I am an obstacle in his path. There be some whose eyes

I have opened to his villany, so that he has lost much credit in certain of the parishes. I doubt not that he will contrive some shrewd stroke for vengeance."

My face fell somewhat, for I am not ashamed to confess that I fear a bad priest, the more so in that I yield to none in my reverence for a good one. I turned my iron sharply in the coals, and then exclaimed:

"Oh, well, we need not greatly trouble ourselves. There are others, methinks, as strong as the Black Abbé, evil though he be!" But I spoke, as I have often found it expedient to do, with more confidence than I felt.

Even at this moment, shrill and clear from the leafage at one end of the forge, came the call of the big yellow-winged woodpecker. I pricked up my ears and stiffened my muscles, expectant of I knew not what.

Marc looked at me with some surprise.

"It's only a woodpecker!" said he.

"But it's only in the spring," I protested, "that he has a cry like that!"

" He cries untimely, as an omen of the ills to come ! " said Marc, half meaning it and half in jest.

Had it been anywhere on the perilous frontier, — on the Richelieu or in the West, or nigh the bloody Massachusetts line, my suspicions would have sprung up wide awake. But in this quiet land between the Habitants and the Canard I was off my guard, — and what a relief it was, indeed, to let myself be careless for a little ! I thought no more of the woodpecker, but remembered that sister with the red hair. I came back to her by indirection, however.

" And how did you manage, lad, to be seeing Mistress Prudence, and her sister, and the child, and yet no others of the English ? A matter of dark nights and back windows ? Eh ? But come to think of it, there was a clear moon this day four weeks back, when you were at Annapolis."

" No, Father," answered Marc, " it was all much more simple and less adventurous than that. Some short way out of the town is a little river, the Equille, and a pleasant hidden glade set high upon its bank. It is a favoured resort of both the ladies; and there I met them as often as I was permitted. Mizpah would sometimes choose to play apart with the child, down by the water's edge if the tide were full, so I had some gracious opportunity with Prudence.—My time being brief, I made the most of it!" he added drily. His quaint directness amused me mightily, and I chuckled as I shaped the red iron upon the anvil.

"And who," I inquired, "is this kind sister, with the even redder hair, who goes away with such a timely discretion?"

"Oh, yes," said Marc, "I forgot you knew nothing of her. She is Mistress Mizpah Hanford, the widow of a Captain Hanford who was some far connection of the Governor's. Her property is in and about Annapolis, and she lives there to manage it, keeping Prudence with her for companionship. Her child is four or five years old, a yellow-haired, rosy boy called Philip. She's very tall,—a head taller than Prudence, and older, of course, by perhaps eight years; and very fair, though not so fair as Prudence; and altogether—"

But at this point I interrupted him.

"What's the matter with the Indian?" I exclaimed, staring out across Marc's shoulders.

He sprang to his feet and looked around sharply. An Indian, carrying three shad strung upon a sapling, had just appeared on the road before the forge door. As he came in view he was reeling heavily, and clutching at his head. He dropped his fish; and a moment later he himself fell headlong, and lay face downward in the middle of the road. I remember thinking that his legs sprawled childishly. Marc strolled over to him with slow indifference.

"Have a care!" I exclaimed. "There may be some trap in it! It looks not natural!"

"What trap can there be?" asked Marc, turning the body over. "It's Red Moose, a Shubenacadie Micmac. I like not the breed; but ever since he got a hurt on the head, in a fight at Canseau last year, he has been subject to the falling sickness. Let us carry him to a shady place, and he'll come to himself presently!"

I was at his side in a moment, and we stooped to lift the seemingly lifeless figure. In an instant its arms were about my neck in a strangling embrace. At the same time my own arms were seized. I heard a fierce cry from Marc, and a groan that was not his. The next moment, though I writhed and struggled with all my strength, I found myself bound hand and foot, and seated on the ground with my back against the door-post of the forge. Marc, bound like myself, lay by the roadside; and a painted savage sat near him nursing with both hands a broken jaw. A dozen Micmacs stood about us. Leaning against the door-post over against me was the black-robed form of La Garne. He eyed me, for perhaps ten seconds, with a smile of fine and penetrating sarcasm. Then he told his followers to stand Marc up against a tree.

Chapter II

The Black Abbé

WHEN first I saw that smile on the Black Abbé's face, and realized what had befallen us, I came nigh to bursting with rage, and was on the point of telling my captor some truths to make his ears tingle. But when I heard the order to stand Marc up against a tree my veins for an instant turned to ice. Many men — and some women, too, God help me, I then being bound and gagged, — had I seen thus stood up against a tree, and never but for one end. I could not believe that such an end was contemplated now, and that by a priest of the Church, however unworthy of his office! But I checked my tongue and spoke the Abbé fair.

"It is quite plain to me, Monsieur,"

said I, quietly, "that my son and I are the victims of some serious mistake, for which you will, I am sure, feel constrained to ask our pardon presently. I await your explanations."

La Garne, still smiling, looked me over slowly. Never before had I seen him face to face, though he had more than once traversed my line of vision. I had known the tireless figure, as tall, almost, as Marc himself, stoop-shouldered, but robust, now moving swiftly as if propelled by an energy irresistible, now languid with an affectation of indolence. But the face —I hated the possessor of it with a personal hate the moment my eyes fell upon that face. Strong and inflexible was the gaunt, broad, and thin jaw, cruel and cunning the high, pinched forehead and narrow-set, palely glinting eyes. The nose, in particular, greatly offended me, being very long, and thick at the end. "I'll tweak it for him, one fine day," says I to myself, as I boiled under his steady smile.

"There is no mistake, Monsieur de Briart, believe me!" he said, still smiling.

There could be no more fair words, of course, after that avowal.

"Then, Sir Priest," said I, coldly, "you are both a madman and a scurvy rogue, and you shall yet be on your knees to me for this outrage. You will see then the nature of your mistake, I give you my word."

The priest's smile took on something of the complexion of a snarl.

"Don't be alarmed, Monsieur de Briart," said he. "You are quite safe, because I know you for a good servant to France; and for your late disrespect to Holy Church, in my person, while in talk with your pestilent son, these bonds may be a wholesome and sufficient lesson to you!"

"You shall have a lesson sufficient rather than wholesome, I promise you!" said I.

"But as for this fellow," went on the Abbé, without noticing my interruption, "he is a spy. You understand how spies fare, Monsieur!" And a malignant light made his eyes appear like two points of steel beneath the ambush of his ragged brows.

I saw Marc's lean face flush thickly under the gross accusation.

"It is a lie, you frocked hound!" he cried, careless of the instant peril in which he stood.

But the Black Abbé never looked at him.

"I wish you joy of your son, a very good Englishman, Monsieur, and now, I fear, not long for this world," said he, in a tone of high civility. "He has long been fouling with his slanders the names of those whom he should reverence, and persuading the people to the English. But now, after patiently waiting, I have proofs. His treachery shall hang him!"

For a moment the dear lad's peril froze my senses, so that it was but dimly I heard his voice, ringing with indignation as he hurled back the charge upon the lying lips that made it.

"If the home of lies be anywhere out of Hell, it is in your malignant mouth, you shame of the Church," he cried in defiance. "There can be no proof that I am a spy, even as there can be no proof that you are other than a false-tongued assassin, defiling your sacred office."

It was the galling defiance of a savage warrior at the stake, and even in my fear my heart felt proud of it. The priest was not galled, however, by these penetrating insults.

"As for the proofs," said he, softly, never looking at Marc, but keeping his eyes on my face, "Monsieur de Ramezay shall judge whether they be proofs or not. If he say they are not, I am content."

At a sign, a mere turn of his head it seemed to me, the Indians loosed Marc's feet to lead him away.

"Farewell, Father," said he, in a firm voice, and turned upon me a look of unshakable courage.

"Be of good heart, son," I cried to him. "I will be there, and this devil shall be balked!"

"You, Monsieur," said the priest, still smiling, "will remain here for the present.

To-night I will send a villager to loose your bonds. Then, by all means, come over and see Monsieur de Ramezay at Chignecto. I may not be there then myself, but this business of the spy will have been settled, for the commander does not waste time in such small matters !"

He turned away to follow his painted band, and I, shaking in my impotent rage and fear, called after him : —

"As God lives and is my witness, if the lad comes to any harm, these hands will visit it upon you an hundredfold, till you scream for death's mercy !"

But the Black Abbé moved off as if he heard no word, and left me a twisted heap upon the turf, gnawing fiercely at the tough deer-hide of my bonds.

Chapter III

Tamin's Little Stratagem

I HAD been gnawing, gnawing in an anguish at the thongs, for perhaps five minutes. There had been no more than time for the Abbé's wolf-pack to vanish by a turn of the road. Suddenly a keen blade slit the thongs that bound my wrists. Then my feet felt themselves free. I sat up, astonished, and saw stooping over me the droll, broad face of Tamin the Fisher, — or Tamin Violet, as he was rightly, though seldom, called. His mouth was solemn, as always, having never been known to wear a smile; but the little wrinkles laughed about his small bright eyes. I sprang up and grasped his hand.

"We must not lose a moment, Tamin, my friend!" I panted, dragging him into the thick shade of the wood.

"I was thinking you might be in a hurry, M'sieu," said my rescuer. "But unless the mouse wants to be back in the same trap I've just let it out of, you'd better keep still a half-minute and make up your mind. They've a round road to go, and we'll go straight!"

"You saw it all?" I asked, curbing myself as best I could, for I perceived the wisdom of his counsel.

"Oh, ay, M'sieu, I saw it!" replied the Fisher. "And I laughed in my bones to hear the lad talk up to the good father. There was more than one shot went home, I warrant, for all the Black Abbé seemed so deaf. They're festering under his soutane even now, belike!"

"But come!" said I. "I've got my wind!" And we darted noiselessly through the cool of the great trees, turning a little east from the road.

We ran silently for a space, my companion's short but massive frame leaping, bending, gliding even as lightly as my own, which was ever as lithe as a weasel's. Tamin was a rare woodsman, as I marked straightway, though I had known him of old rather as a faithful tenant, and marvellously patient to sit in his boat all day a-fishing on the drift of the Minas tides.

Presently he spoke, under his breath.

"Very like," said he, drily, "when we come up to them they will all fall down. So, we will take the lad and walk away! eh, what, M'sieu?"

"Only let us come up to them," said I, "and learn their plans. Then we will make ours!"

"Something of theirs I know," said Tamin. "Their canoes are on the Canard maybe three furlongs to east of the road. Thence they will carry the lad to de Ramezay, for the Black Abbé will have things in due form when he can conveniently, and now it is plain he has a scheme well ripe. But if this wind holds, we'll be there before them. My boat is lying hard by."

"God be praised!" I muttered; for in truth I saw some light now for the first time.   Presently, drawing near the road again, I heard the voice of La Garne.   We at once went softly, and, avoiding again, made direct for where lay the canoes. There we disposed ourselves in a swampy thicket, with a little breadth of water lying before and all the forest behind. The canoes lay just across the little water, and so close that I might have tossed my cap into them.   The clean smell of the wet salt sedge came freshly into the thicket.   The shadows lay long on the water.   We had time to grow quiet, till our breathing was no longer hasty, our blood no longer thumped in our ears.   A flock of sand-pipers, with thin cries, settled to feed on the red clay between the canoes and the edge of the tide.   Suddenly they got up, and puffed away in a flicker of white breasts and brown wings; and I laid a hand on Tamin's shoulder.   The painted band, Marc in their midst, La Garne in front, were coming down the slope.

The lad's face was stern and scornful. To my joy I saw that there was to be no immediate departure. The redskins flung themselves down indolently. The Black Abbé saw his prisoner made fast to a tree, and then, telling his followers that he had duties at Pereau which would keep him till past sunset, strode off swiftly up the trail. Tamin and I, creeping as silently as snakes back into the forest, followed him.

For half an hour we followed him, keeping pace for pace through the shadow of the wood. Then said I softly to Tamin : —

"This is my quarrel, my friend! Do you keep back, and not bring down his vengeance on your head."

"That for his vengeance!" whispered Tamin, with a derisive gesture. "I will take service with de Ramezay, as a regular soldier of France!"

"Even there," said I, "his arm might reach and pluck you forth. Keep back now, and let him not see your face!"

"Priest though he be, M'sieu," urged Tamin, anxiously, "he is a mighty man of his hands!"

I turned upon him a face of scorn which he found sufficient answer. Then, signing to him to hold off, I sped forward silently. No weapon had I but a light stick of green ash, just cut. There was smooth, mossy ground along the trail, and my running feet made no more sound than a cat's. I was within a pace of springing upon his neck, when he must have felt my coming. He turned like a flash, uttered a piercing signal cry, and whipped out a dagger.

" They'll never hear it," mocked I, and sent the dagger spinning with a smart pass of my stick. The same stroke went nigh to breaking his wrist. He grappled bravely, however, as I took him by the throat, and I was astonished at his force and suppleness. Nevertheless the struggle was but brief, and the result a matter to be sworn to beforehand; for I, though not of great stature, am stronger than any other man, big or little, with whom I have ever come to trial; and more than that, when I was a prisoner among the English, I learned their shrewd fashion of wrestling. In a little space the Black Abbé lay choked into submission, after which I bound him in a way to endure, and seated him against a tree. Behind him I caught view of Tamin, gesturing drolly, whereat I laughed till I marked an amazement growing in the priest's malignant eyes.

"How like you my lesson, good Father?" I inquired.

But he only glared upon me. I suppose, having no speech that would fitly express his feelings, he conceived that his silence would be most eloquent. But I could see that my next move startled him. With my knife I cut a piece from my shirt, and made therewith a neat gag.

"Though you seem so dumb at this present," said I, "I suspect that you might find a tongue after my departure. Therefore I must beseech you to wear this ornament, for my sake, for a little." And very civilly prying his teeth open, I adjusted the gag.

"Do not be afraid!" I continued. "I will leave you in this discomfort no longer than you thought it necessary to leave me so. You shall be free after to-morrow's sunrise, if not before. Farewell, good Father, and may you rest well! Let me borrow this ring as a pledge for the safe return of the fragment of my good shirt which you hold so obstinately between your teeth!" And drawing his ring from his finger I turned away and plunged into the forest, where Tamin presently joined me.

Tamin chuckled, deep in his stomach.

"My turn now!" said he. "Give me the ring, M'sieu, and I'll give you the boy!"

"I see you take me!" said I, highly pleased at his quick discernment.

We now made way at leisure back to the canoes, and our plans ripened as we went.

Before we came within hearing of the Indians I gave over the ring with final directions, to Tamin, and then hastened toward the point of land which runs far out beyond the mouth of the Habitants. Around this point, as I knew, lay the little creek-mouth wherein Tamin kept his boat. Beyond the point, perchance a furlong, was a narrow sand-spit covered deep at every flood tide. In a thicket of fir bushes on the bluff over against this sand-spit I lay down to wait for what Tamin should bring to pass. I had some little time to wait; and here let me unfold, as I learned it after, what Tamin did whilst I waited.

About sunset, the tide being far out, and the Indians beginning to expect their Abbé's return, came Tamin to them running in haste along the trail from Pereau, as one who carried orders of importance. Going straight to the chief, he pointed derisively at Marc, whose back was towards him, and cried : —

"The good father commands that you take this dog of a spy straightway to the sand-spit that lies off the point yonder. There you will drive a strong stake into the sand, and bind the fellow to it, and leave him there, and return here to await the Abbé's coming. You shall do no hurt to the spy, and set no mark upon him. When the tide next ebbs you will go again to the sand-spit and bring his body back; and if the Abbé finds any mark upon him, you will get no pay for this venture. You will make your camp here to-night, and if the good father be not returned to you by sunrise to-morrow, you will go to meet him along the Pereau trail, for he will be in need of you."

The tall chief grunted, and eyed him doubtfully. After a brief contemplation he inquired, in broken French : —

" How know you no lie to me ? "

" Here is the holy father's ring, in warranty ; and you shall give it back to him when he comes."

" It is well," said the chief, taking the ring, and turning to give some commands in his own guttural tongue. Tamin repeated his message word by word, then strode away ; and before he got out of sight he saw two canoes put off for the sand-spit. Then he made all haste to join me on the point.

Long before he arrived the canoes had come stealing around the point and were drawn up on the treacherous isle of sand.

"HIS HEAD DROOPED FORWARD UPON HIS BREAST"

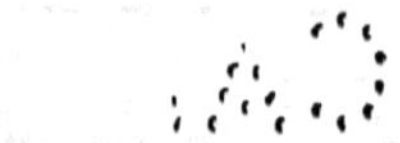

My heart bled for the horror of death which, as I knew, must now be clutching at Marc's soul; but I kept telling myself how soon I would make him glad. It wanted yet three hours or more till the tide should cover the sand-spit. I lay very still among the young fir trees, so that a wood-mouse ran within an arm's length of my face, till it caught the moving of my eyes and scurried off with a frightened squeak. I heard the low change in the note of the tide as the first of the flood began to creep in upon the weeds and pebbles. Then with some farewell taunts, to which Marc answered not a word, the savages went again to their canoes and paddled off swiftly.

When they had become but specks on the dim water, I doffed my clothes, took my knife between my teeth, and swam across to the sand-spit. There was a low moon, obscured by thin and slowly drifting clouds, and as I swam through the faint trail of it, Marc must have seen me coming. Nevertheless he gave no sign, and I could see that his head drooped forward upon his breast.   An awful fear came down upon me, and for a second or two I was like to sink, so numb I turned at the thought that perchance the savages had put the knife to him before quitting.   I recovered, however, as I called to mind the orders which Tamin had rehearsed to me ere starting on his venture; for I knew how sorely the Black Abbé was feared by his savage flock.   What they deemed him to have commanded, that would they do.

Drawing closer now, I felt the ground beneath my feet.

"Marc," I called softly, " I'm coming, lad!"

The drooped head was lifted.

"Father!" he exclaimed.   And there was something like a sob in that cry of joy.   It caught my heart strangely, telling me he was still a boy for all he had borne himself so manfully in the face of sudden and appalling peril.   Now the long tension was loosed.   He was alone with me. As I sprang to him and cut the thongs that held him, one arm went about my

neck and I was held very close for the
space of some few heart-beats. Then he
fetched a deep breath, stretched his cramped
limbs this way and that, and said simply,
" I knew you would come, Father! I
knew you would find a way!"

Chapter IV

The Governor's Signature

THE clouds slipped clear of the moon's face, and we three — Marc, I, and the stake — cast sudden long black shadows which led all the way down to the edge of the increeping tide. I looked at the shadows, and a shudder passed through me as if a cold hand had been laid upon my back. Marc stood off a little, — never have I seen such quick control, such composure, in one so inexperienced, — and remarked to me : —

"What a figure of a man you are, Father, to be sure!"

I fell into his pretence of lightness at once, a high relief after the long and deadly strain ; and I laughed with some pleasure at the praise. In very truth, I cherished a secret pride in my body.

"'Tis well enough, no doubt, in a dim light," said I, "though by now surely somewhat battered!"

Marc was already taking off his clothes. As he knotted them into a convenient bundle, there came from the woods, a little way back of the point, the hollow "Too-hoo-hoo-whoo-oo!" of the small gray owl.

"There's Tamin!" said I, and was on the point of answering in like fashion, when the cry was reiterated twice.

"That means danger, and much need of haste for us," I growled. Together we ran down into the tide, striking out with long strokes for the fine white line that seethed softly along the dark base of the point. I commended the lad mightily for his swimming, as we scrambled upon the beach and slipped swiftly into our clothes. Though carrying his bundle on his head, he had given me all I could do to keep abreast of him.

We climbed the bluff, and ran through the wet, keen-scented bushes toward the creek where lay the boat. Ere we had gone half-way Tamin met us, breathless.

"What danger?" I asked.

"I think they're coming back to tuck the lad in for the night, and see that he's comfortable!" replied Tamin, panting heavily. "I heard paddles when they should have been long out of earshot."

"Something has put them in doubt!" said Marc.

"Sure," said I, "and not strange, if one but think of it!"

"Yet I told them a fair tale," panted Tamin, as he went on swiftly toward his boat.

The boat lay yet some yards above the edge of tide, having been run aground near high water. The three of us were not long in dragging her down and getting her afloat. Then came the question that was uppermost.

"Which way?" asked Tamin, laconically, taking the tiller, while Marc stood by to hoist the dark and well-patched sail.

I considered the wind for some moments.

"For Chignecto!" said I, with emphasis. "We must see de Ramezay and settle this hound La Garne. Otherwise Marc stands in hourly peril."

As the broad sail drew, and the good boat, leaning well over, gathered way, and the small waves swished and gurgled merrily under her quarter, I could hardly withhold from laughing for sheer gladness. Marc was already smoking with great composure beside the mast, his lean face thoughtful, but untroubled. He looked, I thought, almost as old as his war-battered sire who now watched him with so proud an eye. Presently I heard Tamin fetch a succession of mighty breaths, as he emptied and filled the ample bellows of his lungs. He snatched the green and yellow cap of knitted wool from his head, and let the wind cool the sweating black tangle that coarsely thatched his broad skull.

"Hein!" he exclaimed, with a droll glance at Marc, "that's better than *that!*" And he made an expressive gesture as of setting a knife to his scalp. To me this

seemed much out of place and time; but
Tamin was ever privileged in the eyes of
a de Mer, so I grumbled not. As for
Marc, that phantom of a smile, which I
had already learned to watch for, just
touched his lips, as he remarked calmly:

"Vraiment, much better. That, as you
call it, my Tamin, came so near to-night
that my scalp needs no cooling since!"

"But whither steering?" I inquired;
for the boat was speeding south-eastward,
straight toward Grand Pré.

Tamin's face told plainly that he had
his reasons, and I doubted not that they
were good. For some moments that
wide, grave mouth opened not to make
reply, while the little, twinkling, contra-
dictory eyes were fixed intently on some
far-off landmark, to me invisible. This
point being made apparently to his satisfaction, he relaxed and explained.

"You see, M'sieu," said he, "we must
get under the loom o' the shore, so's we'll
be out of sight when the canoes come round
the point. If they see a sail, at this time
o' night, they'll suspicion the whole thing

and be after us. Better let 'em amuse themselves for a spell hunting for the lad on dry land, so's we won't be rushed. Been enough rush!"

"Yes! Yes!" assented I, scanning eagerly the point behind us. And Marc said:—

"Very great is your sagacity, my Tamin. The Black Abbé fooled himself when he forgot to take you into his reckoning!"

At this speech the little wrinkles gathered thicker about Tamin's eyes. At length, deeming us to have gone far enough to catch the loom of the land, as it lay for one watching from the sand-spit, Tamin altered our course, and we ran up the basin. Just then we marked two canoes rounding the point. They were plainly visible to us, and I made sure we should be seen at once; but a glance at Tamin's face reassured me. The Fisher understood, as few even among old woodsmen understand it, the lay of the shadow-belts on a wide water at night.

Noiselessly we lowered our sail and lay drifting, solicitous to mark what the savages might do. The sand-spit was by this so small that from where we lay it was not to be discerned; but we observed the Indians run their canoes upon it, disembark, and stoop to examine the footprints in the sand. In a moment or two they embarked again, and paddled straight to the point.

"Shrewd enough!" said Marc.

"Yes," said I, "and now they'll track us straight to Tamin's creek, and understand that we've taken the boat. But they won't know what direction we've taken!"

"No, M'sieu," muttered Tamin, "but no use loafing round here till they find out!"

Which being undoubted wisdom of Tamin's, we again hoisted sail and continued our voyage.

Having run some miles up the Basin, we altered our course and stood straight across for the northern shore. We now felt secure from pursuit, holding it highly improbable that the savages would guess our purpose and destination. As we sat contenting our eyes with the great bellying of the sail, and the fine flurries of spray that ever and again flashed up from our speeding prow, and the silver-blue creaming of our wake, Marc gave us a surprise. Thrusting his hand into the bosom of his shirt he drew out a packet and handed it to me.

" Here, perhaps, are the proofs on which the gentle Abbé relied !" said he.

Taking the packet mechanically, I stared at the lad in astonishment. But there was no information to be gathered from that inscrutable countenance, so I presently recollected myself, and unfolded the papers. There were two of them. The moon was partly clear at the moment, and I made out the first to be an order, written in English, on one Master Nathaniel Apthorp, merchant, of Boston, directing him to pay Master Marc de Mer, of Grand Pré in Nova Scotia, the sum of two hundred and fifty pounds. It was signed " Paul Mascarene, Govr of Nova Scotia." The other paper was written in finer and more hasty characters, and I could not decipher it in the uncertain light. But the signature was the same as that appended to the order on Mr. Apthorp.

"I cannot decipher this one, in this bad light," said I; "but what does it all mean, Marc? How comes the English Governor to be owing you two hundred and fifty pounds?"

"Does he owe me two hundred and fifty pounds? That's surely news of interest!" said Marc.

I looked at him, amazed.

"Do you mean to say that you don't know what is in these papers?" I inquired, handing them back.

"How should I know that?" said Marc, with a calmness which was not a little irritating. "They were placed in my pocket by the good Abbé; and since then my opportunities of reading have been but scant!"

Tamin ejaculated a huge grunt of indignant comprehension; and I, beholding all at once the whole wicked device, threw up my hands and fell to whistling an idle air. It seemed to me a case for which curses would seem but tame and pale.

" This other, then," said I, presently, " must be a letter that would seem to have been written to you by the Governor, and worded in such a fashion as to compromise you plainly ! "

" 'Tis altogether probable, Father," replied Marc, musingly, as he scanned the page. He was trying to prove his own eyesight better than mine, but found the enterprise beyond him, — as I knew he would.

" I can make out nothing of this other, save the signature," he continued. " We must even wait for daylight. And in the meanwhile I think you had better keep the packet, Father, for I feel my wits and my experience something lacking in this snarl."

I took the papers and hid them in a deep pocket which I wore within the bosom of my shirt.

" The trap was well set, and deadly, lad," said I, highly pleased at his confidence in my wisdom to conduct the affair. " But trust me to spring it. Whatever this other paper may contain, de Ramezay shall see them both and understand the whole plot."

" 'Twill be hard to explain away," said Marc, doubtfully, " if it be forged with any fair degree of skill ! "

" Trust my credit with de Ramezay for that.   It is something the Black Abbé has not reckoned upon ! " said I, with assurance, stuffing my pipe contentedly with the right Virginia leaf.   Marc, being well tired with all that he had undergone that day, laid his head on the cuddy and was presently sound asleep.   In a low voice, not to disturb the slumberer, I talked with Tamin, and learned how he had chanced to come so pat upon me in my bonds. He had been on the way up to the Forge, coming not by the trail, but straight through the forest, when he caught a view of the Indians, and took alarm at the stealth of their approach.   He had tracked them with a cunning beyond their own, and so achieved to outdo them with their own weapons.

The moon now swam clear in the naked sky, the clouds lying far below.   By the

broad light I could see very well to read
the letter. It was but brief, and ran
thus : —

*To my good Friend and trusted Helper Monsieur
Marc de Mer : —*

DEAR SIR,—As touching the affair which
you have so prudently carried through, and my
gratitude for your so good help, permit the en-
closed order on Master Apthorp to speak for
me. If I might hope that you would find it in
your heart and within your convenience to put
me under yet weightier obligations, I would be
so bold as to desire an exact account of the
forces at Chignecto, and of the enterprize upon
which Monsieur de Ramezay is purposing to
employ them.

Believe me to be, my dear Sir, yours with
high esteem and consideration,

PAUL MASCARENE.

With a wonder of indignation I read it
through, and then again aloud to Tamin,
who cursed the author with such ingenious
Acadian oaths as made me presently smile.

"It is right shrewdly devised," said I,
"but the deviser knew little of the blunt

English Governor, or never would he have made him write with such courtly circumlocutions. De Ramezay, very like, will have seen communications of Mascarene's before now, and will scarce fail to note the disagreement."

"The fox has been known to file his tongue too smooth," said Tamin, sententiously.

By this we were come over against the huge black front of Blomidon, but our course lay far outside the shadow of his frown, in the silvery run of the seas. The moon floated high over the great Cape, yellow as gold, and the bare sky was like an unruffled lake. Far behind us opened the mouth of the Piziquid stream, a bright gap in the dark but vague shore-line. On our right the waters unrolled without obstruction till they mixed pallidly with the sky in the mouth of Cobequid Bay. Five miles ahead rose the lofty shore which formed the northern wall of Minas Channel, — grim and forbidding enough by day; but now, in such fashion did the moonlight fall along it, wearing a face of fairyland, and hinting of fountained palaces in its glens and high hollows. After I had filled my heart with the fairness and the wonder of it, I lay down upon a thwart and fell asleep.

Chapter V

In the Run of the Seas

IT seemed as if I had but fairly got my eyes shut, when I was awakened by a violent pitching of the boat. I sat up, grasping the gunwale, and saw Marc just catching my knee to rouse me. The boat, heeling far over, and hauled close to the wind, was heading a little up the channel and straight for a narrow inlet which I knew to be the joint mouth of two small rivers.

"Where are you going? Why is our course changed?" I asked sharply, being nettled by a sudden notion that they had made some change of plan without my counsel.

"Look yonder, Father!" said Marc, pointing.

I looked, and my heart shook with

mingled wrath and apprehension. Behind us followed three canoes, urged on by sail and paddle.

"They outsail us?" I inquired.

"Ay, before the wind, they do, M'sieu!" said Tamin. "On this tack, maybe not. We'll soon see!"

"But what's this but a mere trap we are running our heads into?" I urged.

"I fear there's nothing else but to quit the boat and make through the woods, Father," explained Marc; "that is, if we're so fortunate as to keep ahead till we reach land."

"In the woods, I suppose, we can outwit them or outfoot them," said I; "but those Micmacs are untiring on the trail."

"I know a good man with a good boat over by Shulie on the Fundy shore," interposed Tamin. "And I know the way over the hills. We'll cheat the rogue of a priest yet!" And he shrewdly measured the distance that parted us from our pursuers.

"It galls me to be running from these dogs!" I growled.

"Our turn will come," said Marc, glowering darkly at the canoes. "Do you guess the Black Abbé is with them?"

"Not he!" grunted Tamin.

"Things may happen this time," said I, "and the good father may wish to keep his soutane clear of them. It's all plain enough to me now. The Indians, finding themselves tricked, have gone back on the Pereau trail and most inopportunely have released the gentle Abbé from his bonds. He has seen through our game, and has sent his pack to look to it that we never get to de Ramezay. But *he* will have no hand in it. Oh, no!"

"What's plain to me now," interrupted Tamin, with some anxiety in his voice, "is that they're gaining on us fast. They've put down leeboards; an' with leeboards down a Micmac canoe's hard to beat."

"Oh!" I exclaimed bitterly, "if we had but our muskets! Fool that I was, thus to think to save time and not go back for our weapons! Trust me,

lad, it's the first time that Jean de Mer
has had that particular kind of folly to
repent of!"

"But there was nought else for it,"
Father," said Marc. "And if, as seems
most possible, we come to close quarters
presently, we are not so naked as we
might be. Here's your two pistols, my
good whinger, and Tamin's fishy dirk.
And Tamin's gaff here will make a
pretty lance. It is borne in upon me
that some of the good Abbé's lambs will
bleat for their shepherd before this night's
work be done!"

There was a steady light in his eyes
that rejoiced me much, and his voice rose
and fell as if fain to break into a war
song; and I said to myself, "The boy
is a fighter, and the fire is in his blood,
for all his scholar's prating of peace!"
Yet he straightway turned his back upon
the enemy and with great indifference went
to filling his pipe.

"Ay, an' there be a right good gun in
the cuddy!" grunted Tamin, after a second or two of silence.

"The saints be praised!" said I. And Marc's long arm reached in to capture it. It was a huge weapon, and my heart beat high at sight of it. Marc caressed it for an instant, then reluctantly passed it to me, with the powder-horn.

" I can shoot, a little, myself," said he, " but I would be presumptuous to boast when you were by, Father!"

"' Ay, vraiment," said Tamin, sharply ; "don't think you can shoot with the Sieur de Briart yet!"

" I don't," replied Marc, simply, as he handed me out a pouch of bullets and a pouch of slugs.

The pursuing canoes were by this come within fair range. There came a strident hail from the foremost : —

" Lay to, or we shoot!"

"Shoot, dogs!" I shouted, ramming home the good measure of powder which I had poured into my hand. I followed it with a fair charge of slugs, and was wadding it loosely, when —

" Duck!" cries Tamin, bobbing his head lower than the tiller.

"THE RESULT OF THE SHOT WAS ALL THAT WE COULD DESIRE"

Neither Marc nor I moved a hair. But we gazed at the canoes. On the instant two red flames blazed out, with a redoubled bang; and one bullet went through the sail a little above my head.

"Not bad!" said Marc, glancing tranquilly at the bullet hole.

But for my own part, I was angry. To be fired upon thus, at a priest's orders, by a pack of scurvy savages in the pay of our own party, — never before had Jean de Briart been put to such indignity. I kneeled, and took a very cautious aim, — not, however, at the savages, but at the bow of the nearest canoe.

Tamin's big gun clapped like a cannon, and kicked my shoulder very vilely. But the result of the shot was all that we could desire. As I made haste to load again I noticed that the savage in the bow had fallen backward in his place, hit by a stray slug. The bulk of the charge, however, had torn a great hole in the bark, close to the water-line.

"You've done it, Father!" said Marc, in a tone of quiet exultation.

"Hein!" grunted Tamin. "They don't like the wet!"

The canoe was going down by the bow. The other two craft ranged hurriedly alongside, and took in the gesticulating crew,—all but one, whom they left in the stern to paddle the damaged canoe to land, being loth to lose a serviceable craft. With broken bow high in air the canoe spun around, and sped off up the Basin before the wind. The remaining two resumed the chase of us. We had gained a great space during the confusion, yet they came up upon us fast.

But now, ere I judged them to be within gunshot, they slackened speed.

"They think better of it!" said I, raising the gun again to my shoulder. As I did so they sheered off in haste to a safer distance.

"They are not such fools as I had hoped!" said Marc.

"I so far flatter myself as to think," said I, with some complacency, "that they won't trust themselves willingly again within range of this good barker."

By this we were come well within the wide mouth of the estuary, and a steep, wooded point thrust out upon our right. All at once I muttered a curse upon my dulness.

"What fools we are, to be sure!" I cried. "No reason that we should toil across the mountains to your good man's good boat at Shulie, my Tamin. Put her about, and we'll sail in comfort around to Chignecto; and let these fellows come in range again at their peril!"

"To be sure, indeed!" grunted Tamin; and with a lurch and great flapping we went about.

The canoes, indeed, now fled before us with excellent discretion. Our new course carried us under the gloom of the promontory, whence, in a few minutes, we shot out again into the moonlight. It was pleasant to see our antagonists making such courteous haste to give us room. I could not forbear to chuckle over it, and wished mightily that the Black Abbé were in one of the canoes.

"I fear me there's to be no work for

Tamin's fishy dirk or my good whinger,"
sighed Marc, with a nice air of melan-
choly; and Tamin, with the little wrinkles
thicker than ever about his eyes, yelled
droll taunts after our late pursuers.   In
fact, we were all three in immense high
feather, — when on a sudden there came a
crashing bump that tumbled us headlong,
the mast went overboard, and there we
were stuck fast upon a sharp rock.   The
boat was crushed in like an egg-shell, and
lay over on her side.   The short, chop-
ping seas huddled upon us in a smother.
As I rose up, sputtering, I took note of
Tamin's woollen cap washing away debo-
nairly, snatched off, belike, by a taut rope
as the mast fell.   Then, clinging all three
to the topmost gunwale, the waves jump-
ing and sousing us derisively, we stared at
each other in speechless dismay.   But a
chorus of triumphant screeches from the
canoes, as they noted our mishap and made
to turn, brought us to our senses.

"Nothing for it but to swim!" said I,
thrusting down the now useless musket
into the cuddy, where I hoped it might

stay in case the wrecked boat should drift ashore. It was drenched, of course, and something too heavy to swim with. I emptied the slugs from my pocket. Tamin ducked his head under water and fumbled in the cuddy till I was on the point of plucking him forth, fearing he would drown, — Marc, meanwhile, looking on tranquilly and silently, with that fleeting remembrance of a smile. But now Tamin arose, gasping, with a small sack and a salted hake in his hands. The fish he passed over to me.

"Bread, M'sieu!" said he, holding up the drenched sack in triumph. "Now for the woods!"

'Twas but the toss of a biscuit to shore, and we had gained it ere our enemies were come within gunshot. Running swiftly along the strip of beach that skirted the steep, we put the shoulder of the cape between, and were safe from observation for a few minutes.

"To the woods, M'sieu!" cried Tamin, in a suppressed voice.

"No!" said I, sternly. "Straight

along the beach, till I give the word to turn in!   Follow me!"

"'Tis the one chance, to get out of sight now!" grumbled Tamin, running beside me, and clutching at his wet sack of bread.

"Don't you suppose he knows what he is doing, my Tamin?" interrupted Marc. "'Tis for you and me to obey orders!"

Tamin growled, but said no more.

"Now in with you to cover," I commanded, waving my salt fish as it had been a marshal's baton. At the same moment I turned, ran up the wet slope where a spring bubbled out of the wood's edge and spread itself over the stones, and sprang behind a thick screen of viburnums. My companions were beside me on the instant, — but it was not an instant too soon. As we paused to look back, there were the canoes coming furiously around the point.

Staying not long to observe them, I led the way straight into the darkness of the woods, aiming for the seashore at the other side of the point. But Tamin was not satisfied.

"Our road lies straight up yon river," said he.

"My friend," said I, "we must e'en find another road to Shulie. Those fellows will be sure to agree that we have gone that way. Knowing that I am a cunning woodsman, they will say, ' He will make them to run in the water, and so leave no trail.' And they will give hot chase up the river."

"But there be two rivers," objected Tamin.

"Bien," said I, "they will divide their party, and give hot chase up two rivers !"

"And in the meanwhile ?" inquired Marc.

"I'll find the way to Shulie," said I. "The stars and the sun are guide enough ! I know the main lay of all these coasts."

Chapter VI

Grûl

THE undergrowth into which we had now come was thick and hindering, so there was no further chance of speech. A few minutes more and we came out upon the seaward slope of the point. We pushed straight down to the water, here sheltered from the wind and little troubled. That our footprints might be hidden, at least for a time, we ran, one behind the other, along the lip of the tide, where the water was about ankle deep. In the stillness our splashing sounded dangerously loud, and Tamin, yet in a grumbling humour, spoke of it.

"But you forget, my friend," said I, gently, "that there is noise and to spare where our enemies are, — across there in the wind!"

In a moment Tamin spoke again, pointing some little way ahead.

"The land drops away yonder, M'sieu, 'twixt the point and the main shore!" he growled, with conspicuous anxiety in his voice. He was no trembler; but it fretted him to be taking what he deemed the weaker course. "Nothing," he added, "but a bit of bare beach that the waves go over at spring tides when the wind's down the Basin!"

I paused in some dismay. But my mind was made up.

"We must go on," said I. "But we will stoop low, and lose no time in the passage. They'll scarce be landed yet."

And now, as I came to see how low indeed that strip of perilous beach was, I somewhat misdoubted of success in getting by unseen. But we went a little deeper in the tide, and bowed our bodies with great humbleness, and so passed over with painful effort but not a little speed. Being come again under shelter, we straightened ourselves, well pleased, fetched a deep breath or two, and ran on with fresh celerity.

" But if a redskin should think to step over the beach, there'd be our goose cooked!" muttered Tamin.

" Well said!" I answered. " Therefore let us strike inland at once!" And I led the way again into the darkness of the forest.

Dark as it was, there was yet light enough from the moon to enable me to direct my course as I wished. I struck well west of the course which would have taken us most speedily to Shulie, being determined to avoid the valley of the stream which I considered our pursuers were most likely to ascend. To satisfy Tamin's doubts I explained my purpose, which was to aim straight for Shulie as soon as we were over the water-shed. And I must do him the justice to say he was content, beginning now to come more graciously to my view. We went but slowly, climbing, ever climbing. At times we would be groping through a great blackness of hemlocks. Again the forest would be more open, a mingling of fir trees, and birches, and maples.

Coming at last to more level ground, we were still much hindered by innumerable rocks, amid which the underbrush and wild vines prepared pitfalls for our weary feet. But I was not yet willing to call a halt for breath. On, on we stumbled, the wet branches buffeting our faces, but a cool and pleasant savour of the wild herbs which we trod upon ever exhaling upwards to refresh our senses. As we crossed a little grassy glade, I observed that Marc had come to Tamin's help, and was carrying the sack of bread. I observed, also, that Tamin's face was drawn with fatigue, and that he went with a kind of dogged heaviness. I took pity upon him. We had put, I guessed, good miles between ourselves and our pursuers, and I felt that we were, in all reason, safe for the time. At the further limit of the glade there chattered a shallow brook, whose sweet noise reminded me that I was parched with thirst. The pallor of first dawn was now coming into the sky, and the tree tops began to lift and float in an aërial grayness. I glanced at Marc, and his eyes met mine with a keen brightness that told me he was yet unwearied. Nevertheless I cried: —

"Halt, and fall out for breakfast." And with the words I flung myself down by the brook, thrust my burning face into the babbling chill of it, and drank luxuriously. Tamin was beside me in an instant; but Marc slaked his thirst at more leisure, when he had well enjoyed watching our satisfaction.

We lay for a little, till the sky was touched here and there with saffron and flying wisps of pink, and we began to see the colour of grass and leaves. Then we made our meal, — a morsel each of the salt hake which I had clung to through our flight, and some bits of Tamin's black bread. This bread was wholesome, as I well knew, and to our hunger it was not unsavoury; but it was of a hardness which the sea-water had scarce availed to mitigate.

As we ground hastily upon the meagre fare, I felt, rather than heard, a presence come behind me. I turned my head with a start, and at the same instant heard a high, plangent voice, close beside us, crying slowly : —

" Woe, woe to Acadie the Fair, for the day of her desolation cometh."

It was an astonishing figure upon which my eyes fell, — a figure which might have been grotesque, but was not. Instead of laughing, my heart thrilled with a kind of awe. The man was not old, — his frame was erect and strong with manhood; but the long hair hanging about his neck was white, the long beard streaming upon his half-naked breast was white. He wore leathern breeches, and the upper portion of his body was covered only by a cloak of coarse woollen stuff, woven in a staring pattern of black and yellow. On his head was a rimless cap of plaited straw, with a high, pointed crown; and this was stuck full of gaudy flowers and feathers. From the point of the crown rose the stump of what had been, belike, a spray of golden-rod, broken by a hasty journeying through the obstructions of the forest. The man's eyes, of a wild and flaming blue, fixed themselves on mine. In one hand he carried a white stick, with a grotesque carven head, dyed scarlet, which he pointed straight at me.

" Do you lie down, like cows that chew the cud, when the wolves are on the trail?" demanded that plangent voice.

" It's Grûl!" cried Tamin, springing to his feet and thrusting a piece of black bread into the stranger's hand.

But the offering was thrust aside, while those wide eyes flamed yet more wildly upon me.

" They are on the trail, I tell you!" he repeated. " I hear their feet even now! Go! Run! Fly!" and he stooped, with an ear toward the ground.

" But which way should we fly?" I asked, half in doubt whether his warning should be heeded or derided. I could see that neither Marc nor Tamin had any such doubts. They were on the strain to be off, and only awaited my word.

" Go up the brook," said he, in a lower voice. " The first small stream on your left hand, turn up that a little way, and so — for the wolves shall this time be balked. But the black wolf's teeth bite deep. They shall bite upon the throats of the people!" he continued, his voice rising keenly, his white staff, with its grinning scarlet head, waving in strange, intricate curves. We were already off, making at almost full speed up the brook. Glancing back, I saw the fantastic form running to and fro over the ground where we had lain; and when the trees hid him we heard those ominous words wailed slowly over and over with the reiterance of a tolling bell : —

" Woe, woe for Acadie the Fair, for the day of her desolation cometh ! "

" He'll throw them off the trail ! " said Tamin, confidently.

" But how did they ever get on it ? " queried Marc.

" 'Tis plain that they have seen or heard us as we passed the strip of beach ! " said I, in deep vexation, for I hated to be over-reached by any one in woodcraft. " If we outwit them now, it's no thanks to my tactics, but only to that generous and as-

tonishing madman. You both seemed to
know him. Who, in the name of all the
saints, might he be? What was it you
called him, Tamin?"

"Grûl!" replied Tamin; and said no
more, discreetly husbanding his wind. But
Marc spoke for him.

"I have heard him called no other
name but Grûl! Madman he is, at times,
I think. But sane for the most part, and
with some touches of a wisdom beyond
the wisdom of men. The guise of madness he wears always; and the Indians, as
well as our own people, reverence him
mightily. It is nigh upon three years
since he first appeared in Acadie. He
hates the Black Abbé, — who, they say,
once did him some great mischief in some
other land than this, — and his strange
ravings, his prodigious prophesyings, do
something here and there to weaken the
Abbé's influence with our people."

"Then how does he evade the good
father's wrath?" I questioned, in wonder.

"Oh," said Marc, "the good father
hates him cordially enough. But the

Indians could not be persuaded, or bullied, or bribed, to lift a hand against him. They say a Manitou dwells in him."

" Maybe they're not far wrong!" grunted Tamin.

And now I, like Tamin, found it prudent to spare my wind. But Marc, whose lungs seemed untiring, spoke from time to time as he went, and told me certain incidents, now of Grûl's acuteness, now of his gift of prophecy, now of his fantastic madness. We came at length, after passing two small rivulets on the right, to the stream on the left which Grûl had indicated. It had a firm bed, wherein our footsteps left no trace, and we ascended it for perhaps a mile, by many windings. Then, with crafty care, we crept up from the stream, in such a fashion as to leave no mark of our divergence if, as I thought not likely, our pursuers should come that way. After that we fetched a great circuit, crossed the parent brook, and shortly before noon judged that we might account ourselves secure. Where a tiny spring bubbled beneath a granite boulder and trickled away north toward the Fundy shore, we stopped to munch black bread and the remnant of the fish. We rested for an hour, — Tamin and I sleeping, while Marc, who protested that he felt no motion toward slumber, kept watch. When he roused us, we set off pleasantly refreshed, our faces toward Shulie.

Till late that night we journeyed, having a clear moon to guide us. Coming at length to the edge of a small lake set with islands, " Here," said I, " is the place where we may sleep secure ! "

We stripped, took our bundles on our heads, and swam out into the shining stillness. We swam past two islets, and landed upon one which caught my fancy. There we lay down in a bed of sweet-smelling fern, and were well content. As we supped on Tamin's good black bread, two loons laughed to each other out on the silver surface. We saw their black, watchful heads, moving slowly. Then we slept. It was high day when we awoke. The bread was now scarce, so we husbanded it, and made such good speed all day that while it wanted yet some hours of sunset we came out upon a bluff's edge and saw below us the wash and roll of Fundy. We were some way west of Shulie, but not far, Tamin said, from the house of his good friend with the good boat.

To this house we came within the hour. It was a small, home-like cabin, among apple trees, in a slant clearing that over-hung a narrow creek. There, by a little jetty, I rejoiced to see the boat. The man of the house, one Beaudry, was in the woods looking for his cow, but the good-wife made us welcome. When Beaudry came in he and Tamin fell on each other's necks. And I found, too, that the name of Jean de Briart, with something of his poor exploits, was not all unknown in the cabin.

How well we supped that night, on fresh shad well broiled, and fresh sweet barley bread, and thin brown buckwheat cakes! It was settled at once that Beaudry should put us over to de Ramezay's camp with the first of the morrow's tide. Then, over our pipes, sitting under the apple tree by the porch, we told our late adventures. I say we, but Tamin told them, and gave them a droll colouring which delighted me. It must have tickled Marc's fancy, too, for I took note that he let his pipe out many times during the story. Beaudry kept crying "Hein!" and "Bien!" and "Tiens!" in an ecstasy of admiration. The goodwife, however, was seemingly most touched by the loss of Tamin's knitted cap. With a face of great concern, as who should say "Poor soul!" she jumped up, ran into the house, was gone a few moments, and returned beaming benevolence.

"V'la!" she cried; and stuck upon Tamin's wiry black head a bran-new cap of red wool.

Chapter VII

The Commander is Embarrassed

NEXT day we set out at a good hour, and came without further adventure to Chignecto. Having landed, amid a little swarm of fishing-boats, we then went straight to de Ramezay's headquarters, leaving Beaudry at the wharf among his cronies. We crossed a strip of dyked marsh, whereon were many sleek Acadian cattle cropping the rich aftermath, and ascended the gentle slope of the uplands. Amid a few scattered cabins were ranged the tents of the soldiers. Camp fires and sheaves of stacked muskets gave the bright scene a warlike countenance. Higher up the hill stood a white cottage, larger than the rest, its door painted red, with green panels; and from a staff on its gable, blown out bravely by the wind which ever sweeps those Fundy marsh-lands, flapped the white banner with the Lilies of France.

The sentry who challenged us at the foot of the slope knew me, — had once fought under me in a border skirmish, — and, saluting with great respect, summoned a guard to conduct us to headquarters. As we climbed the last dusty rise and turned in, past the long well-sweep and two gaunt, steeple-like Lombardy poplars, to the yard before the cottage, the door opened and the commander himself stood before us. His face lit up gladly as I stepped forward to greet him, and with great warmth he sprang to embrace me.

"My dear Briart!" he cried. "I have long expected you!"

"I am but just returned to Acadie, my dear friend," said I, with no less warmth than he had evinced, "or you would surely have seen me here to greet you on your coming. But the King's service kept me on the Richelieu!"

"And even your restless activity, my Jean, cannot put you in two places at once," said he, as he turned with an air of courteous inquiry to my companions. Perceiving at once by his dress that Tamin was a habitant, his eyes rested upon Marc.

" My son Marc, Monsieur de Ramezay," said I.

The two bowed, Marc very respectfully, as became a young man on presentation to a distinguished officer, but de Ramezay with a sudden and most noticeable coldness. At this I flushed with anger, but the moment was not one for explanations. I restrained myself; and turning to Tamin, I said in an altered tone : —

" And this, de Ramezay, is my good friend and faithful follower, Tamin Violet, of Canard parish, who desires to enlist for service under you. More of him, and all to his credit, I will tell you by and by. I merely commend him to you now as brave, capable, and a good shot ! "

" I have ever need of such ! " said de Ramezay, quickly. " As you recommend him, he shall serve in Monsieur de Ville d'Avray's company, which forms my own guard."

Summoning an orderly, he gave directions to this effect. As Tamin turned to depart with the orderly, both Marc and I stepped up to him and wrung his hands, and thanked him many times for the courage and craft which had saved Marc's life as well as the honour of our family.

" We'll see you again to-night or in the morning, my Tamin," said Marc.

" And tell you how goes my talk with the commander," added I, quietly.

" And for the boat we wrecked," continued Marc, " why, of course, we won't remain in your debt for a small thing like that; though for the great matter, and for your love, we are always your debtors gladly !"

" And in the King's uniform," said I, cutting short Tamin's attempted protestations, " even the Black Abbé will not try to molest you."

I turned again to de Ramezay, who was waiting a few paces aside, and said, with a courtesy that was something formal after the warmth of our first greeting : —

"Your pardon, de Ramezay! But Tamin has gone through much with us and for us. And now, my son and I would crave an undisturbed conversation with you."

At once, and without a word, he conducted us into his private room, where he invited us to be seated. As we complied, he himself remained standing, with every sign of embarrassment in his frank and fearless countenance. I had ever liked him well. Good cause to like him, indeed, I had in my heart, for I had once stood over his body in a frontier skirmish, and saved his scalp from the knives of the Onondagas. But now my anger was hot against him, for it was plain to me that he had lent ear to some slanders against Marc. For a second or two there was a silence, then Marc sprang to his feet.

"Perhaps if I stand," said he, coldly, "Monsieur de Ramezay will do us the honour of sitting."

De Ramezay's erect figure — a very

soldierly and imposing figure it was in its uniform of white and gold — straightened itself haughtily for an instant. Then he began, but with a stammering tongue: —

"I bitterly regret — it grieves me, — it pains me to even hint it, — " and he kept his eyes upon the floor as he spoke, — "but your son, my dear friend, is accused — "

Here I broke in upon him, springing to my feet.

"Stop!" said I, sternly.

He looked at me with a face of sorrowful inquiry, into which a tinge of anger rose slowly.

"Remember," I continued, "that whatever accusation or imputation you make now, I shall require you to prove beyond a peradventure, — or to make good with your sword against mine! My son is the victim of a vile conspiracy. He is — "

"Then he *is* loyal, you say, to France?" interrupted de Ramezay, eagerly.

"I say," said I, in a voice of steel, "that he has done nothing that his father, a soldier of France, should blush to tell,

—nothing that an honest gentleman should not do." My voice softened a little as I noticed the change in his countenance. "And oh, Ramezay," I continued, "had any man an hour ago told me that *you* would condemn a son of mine unheard, — that you, on the mere word of a false priest or his wretched tools, would have believed that a son of Jean de Mer could be a traitor, I would have driven the words down his throat for a black lie, a slander on my friend!"

De Ramezay was silent for a moment, his eyes fixed upon the floor. Then he lifted his head.

"I was wrong. Forgive me, my friend!" said he, very simply. "I see clearly that I ought to have held the teller of those tales in suspicion, knowing of him what I do know. And now, since you give me your word the tales are false, they are false. Pardon me, I beg of you, Monsieur!" he added, turning to Marc and holding out his hand.

Marc bowed very low, but appeared not to see the hand.

"If you have heard, Monsieur de Ramezay," said he, "that, before it was made plain that France would seek to recover Acadie out of English hands, I, a mere boy, urged my fellow Acadians to accept the rule in good faith;—if you have heard that I then urged them not to be misled to their own undoing by an unscrupulous and merciless intriguer who disgraces his priestly office;—if you have heard that, since then, I have cursed bitterly the corruption at Quebec which is threatening New France with instant ruin,—you have heard but truly!"

De Ramezay bit his lips and flushed slightly. Marc was not making the situation easier; but I could scarce blame him. Our host, however, motioned us to our seats, taking his own chair immediately that he saw us seated. For my own part, my anger was quite assuaged. I hastened to clear the atmosphere.

"Let me tell you the whole story, Ramezay," said I, "and you will understand. But first let me say that my son is wholly devoted to the cause of France.

His former friendly intercourse with the English, a boyish matter, he brought to an utter end when the war came this way."

"And let me say," interrupted de Ramezay, manfully striving to amend his error, "that when one whom I need not name was filling my ear with matter not creditable to a young man named Marc de Mer, it did not come at all to my mind — and can you wonder? — that the person so spoken of was a son of my Briart, of the man who had so perilled his own life to save mine! I thought your son was but a child. It was thus that the accusations were allowed to stick in my mind, — which I do most heartily repent of! And for which I again crave pardon!"

"I beg of you, Monsieur, that you will think no more of it!" said Marc, heartily, being by this quite appeased.

Then with some particularity I told our story, — not omitting Marc's visit to his little Puritan at Annapolis, whereat de Ramezay smiled, and seemed to understand something which had before been dark to him.   When the Black Abbé came upon the scene (I had none of our host's reluctance to mention the Abbé's name !) de Ramezay's brows gathered gloomily. But he heard the tale through with breathless attention up to the point of our landing at Chignecto.

"And now, right glad am I that you are here," he exclaimed, stretching out a hand to each of us.   The frank welcome that illuminated the strong lines of his face left no more shadow of anger in our hearts.

"And here are the Abbé's precious documents !" said I, fetching forth the packet.

De Ramezay examined both letters with the utmost care.

"The reward," he said presently, with a dry smile, "is on a scale that savours of Quebec rather more than of thrifty New England.   When Boston holds the purse-strings, information is bought cheaper than that !   As for the signature, it is passable.   But I fear it would scarce satisfy Master Apthorp !"

"I thought as much," said I, "though I have seen Mascarene's signature but once."

De Ramezay fingered the paper, and held it up to the light.

"But a point which will interest you particularly, Monsieur," he continued, addressing Marc, "is the fact that this paper was made in France!"

"It is gratifying to know that, Monsieur!" replied Marc, with his vanishing smile.

"It would be embarrassing to some people," said de Ramezay, "if they knew we were aware of it. But I may say here frankly that they must not know it. You will readily understand that my hands are something less than free. As things go now at Quebec, there are methods used which I cannot look upon with favour, and which I must therefore seem not to see. I am forced to use the tools which are placed in my hands. This priest of whom you speak is a power in Acadie. He is thought to be indispensable to our cause. He will do the things that, alas, have to be done, but which no one else will do. And I believe he does love France, — he is surely sincere in that. But he rests very heavily, methinks, on the conscience of his good bishop at Quebec, who, but for the powers that interfere, would call him to a sharp account. I tell you all this so that you will see why I must not charge the Abbé with this villany of his. I am compelled to seem ignorant of it."

I assured him that I apprehended the straits in which he found himself, and would be content if he would merely give the Abbé to understand that Marc was not to be meddled with.

"Of course," said Marc, at this point, "I wish to enter active service, with Father; and I shall therefore be, for the most part, beyond the good Abbé's reach. But we have business at Grand Pré and Canard that will hold us there a week or thereabouts; and it is annoying to walk in the hourly peril of being tomahawked and scalped for a spy!"

"I'll undertake to secure you in this

regard," laughed de Ramezay; "and in return, perchance I may count on your support when I move against Annapolis, as my purpose is to do ere many weeks!"

"Assuredly!" said Marc, "if my father have made for me no other plans!" And he turned to me for my word in the matter.

As it chanced, this was exactly as I had purposed, which I made at once to appear. It was presently agreed, therefore, that we should tarry some days at Chignecto, returning thereafter to despatch our affairs at home and await de Ramezay's summons. As the Commander's guests we were lodged in his own quarters, and Tamin was detailed to act as our orderly. The good Beaudry, with his good boat, was sent home not empty-handed to his goodwife near Shulie, with instructions to come again for us in five days. And Tamin, having now no more need of it, sent back to Madame Beaudry, with best compliments, her knitted cap of red wool.

Chapter VIII

The Black Abbé Comes to Dinner

OF the pleasant but something irrelevant matter of how merrily we supped that night with de Ramezay and his officers, — many of whom I knew, all of whom knew me or my adventurous repute, — I will not linger to discourse. Nor of the costly dainties from France which enriched the board, side by side with fair salmon from the Tantramar and bursting-fat plover from the Joli-Cœur marshes. Nor of the good red wine of Burgundy which so enhanced the relish of those delectable birds, — and of which I might perhaps have drunk more sparingly had good Providence but made me more abstemious. Let it suffice to say, there was wit enough to spice plainer fare, and courtesy that had shone at Versailles. The long bare room, with its low, black-raftered ceiling and polished floor, its dark walls patterned with shelves, was lit by the smoky flames of two-score tallow candles.

By and by chairs were pushed back, the company sat with less ceremony, the air grew clouded with the blue vapours of the Virginia weed, and tongues wagged something more loosely than before. There were songs, — catches from the banks of Rhone, rolling ballads of our own voyageurs. A young captain quite lately from Versailles, the Sieur de Ville d'Avray, had an excellent gift of singing.

But now, just when the Sieur de Ville d'Avray was rendering, with most commendable taste and spirit, the ballade of "Frère Lubin," there came an interruption.

> " Il presche en theologien,
>   Mais pour boire de belle eau claire,
>   Faictes la boire a vostre chien,
>   Frère Lubin ne le peult faire," —

sang the gay voice,—we all nodding our heads in intent approval, or even, maybe, seeing that the wine was generous, tapping the measure openly with our fingers. But suddenly, though there was no noise to draw them, all eyes turned to the doorway, and the singer paused in his song. I tipped my chair back into the shadow of a shelf, as did Marc, who sat a little beyond me. For the visitor, who thus boldly entered unannounced, was none other than the Black Abbé himself.

I flung de Ramezay a swift glance of anticipation, which he caught as he arose in his place to greet the new-comer. On the faces around the table I took note of an ill-disguised annoyance. The Abbé, it was plain, found small favour in that company. But to do him justice, he seemed but little careful to court favour. He stood in the doorway, frowning, a piercing and bitter light in his close-set eyes. He waited for de Ramezay to come forward and give him welcome,—which de Ramezay presently did, and would have led him to a seat at the table.

"THE VISITOR . . . WAS NONE OTHER THAN THE BLACK
ABBÉ HIMSELF"

But "No!" said the grim intruder. "With all thanks for your courtesy, Monsieur, I have no time, nor am I in the temper, for revellings. When I have said my word to you I will get me to the house of one of my flock, and sup plainly, and take what rest I may, for at dawn I must set out for the Shubenacadie. There is much to be done, and few to do it, and the time grows short!" and he swept a look of reprimand about the circle.

"Would you speak with me in private, Father?" asked de Ramezay, with great civility.

"It is not necessary, Monsieur!" replied the Abbé. "I have but to say that I arrested the pestilent young traitor, Marc de Mer, on his father's estate at Canard, and left him under guard while I went to attend to other business. I found upon his person clear proofs of his treachery, which would have justified his hanging on the instant. But I preferred that you should be the judge!"

"You did well!" said de Ramezay,

gravely. " I must ask even you, Monsieur l'Abbé, to remember on all occasions that I, and I only, am the judge, so long as I remain in Acadie!"

To this rebuke, courteous though it was, the priest vouchsafed no reply but a slight smile, which uncovered his strong yellow teeth on one side, like a snarl. He continued his report as if there had been no interruption.

" In my brief absence his father, with some disaffected habitants, deceived my faithful followers by a trick, and carried off the prisoner. But I have despatched a strong party on the trail of the fugitives. They will certainly be captured, and brought at once —"

But at this point his voice failed him. His face worked violently with mingled rage and amazement, and following his gaze I saw Marc standing and bowing with elaborate courtesy.

" They are already here, Sir Abbé," said he, " having made haste that they might give you welcome!"

A ripple of laughter went around the

table, as the company, recovering from some moments of astonishment, began to understand the situation. I, too, rose to my feet, smiling expectantly. The priest's narrow eyes met mine for a second, with a light that was akin to madness. Then they shifted. But he found his voice again.

"I denounce that man as a proved spy and traitor!" he shouted, striding forward, and pointing a yellow finger of denunciation across the table at Marc, while the revellers over whom he leaned made way for him resentfully. "I demand his instant arrest."

"Gently, Monsieur l'Abbé," said de Ramezay. "These are serious charges to bring against French gentlemen, and friends of the Commander; have you proofs — such as will convince me after the closest scrutiny?" he added, with unmistakable significance.

"I have myself seen the proofs, I tell you," snarled the Abbé, beginning to exert more self-control, but still far unlike the cool, inexorable, smiling cynic who had

so galled my soul with his imperturba-
bility when I lay in his bonds beside the
Forge.

"I would fain see them, too," insisted
de Ramezay.

The priest glared at me, and then at
Marc, baffled.

"I have them not," said he, in his slow
and biting tones; "but if you would do
your duty as the King's servant, Monsieur
de Ramezay, and arrest yonder spy, you
would doubtless find the proofs upon his
person, if he has not taken the pains to
dispose of them."   Upon this insolent
speech, de Ramezay took his seat, and
left the priest standing alone.   When,
after a pause, he spoke, his voice was
stern and masterful, as if he were addressing a contumacious servant, though he
retained the forms of courtesy in his
phrases.

"Monsieur," said he, "when I wish to
learn my duty, it will not be the somewhat well-known Abbé la Garne whom I
will ask to teach me.   I must require you
not to presume further upon the sacred-

ness of your office. Your soutane saves you from being called to account by the gentleman whose honour you have aspersed. Monsieur Marc de Mer is the son of my friend. He is also one of my aides-de-camp. I beg that you will understand me without more words when I say that I have examined the whole matter to which you refer. For your own credit, press it no further. I trust you catch my meaning!"

"On the contrary," said the Abbé, coolly, being by this time quite himself again, and seemingly indifferent to the derisive faces confronting him — "on the contrary, your meaning altogether escapes me, Monsieur. All that I understand of your singular behaviour is what the Governor and the Intendant, not I their unworthy instrument, will be called to pass judgment upon."

"I will trouble you to understand also, Sir Priest," said de Ramezay, thoroughly aroused, his tones biting like acid, "that if this young man is further troubled by any of your faithful Shubenacadie flock, I will hold you responsible; and the fact that you are useful, having fewer scruples than trouble a mere layman, shall not save you."

" Be not disturbed for your spy, Monsieur," sneered the Abbé, now finely tranquil. " I wash my hands of all responsibility in regard to him; look you to that."

For the space of some seconds there was silence all about that table of feasting, while the Abbé swept a smiling, bitter glance around the room. Last, his eyes rested upon mine and leaped with a sudden light of triumph, so that one might have thought not he but I had been worsted in the present encounter. Then he turned on his heel and went out, scornful of courtesy.

A clamour of talk arose upon this most cherished departure; but I heard it as in a dream, being wrapped up in wonder as to the meaning of that look of triumph.

" Has the Black Abbé cast a spell upon you, Father?" I heard Marc inquiring presently. Whereupon I came to myself with a kind of start, and made merry with the rest of them.

It was late when Marc and I went to the little chamber where our pallets were stretched. There we found Tamin awaiting us. He was in a sweat of fear.

" What is it, my Tamin ? " asked Marc.

" The Black Abbé," he grunted, the drollness all chased out of the little wrinkles about his eyes.

" Well," said I, impatiently. " The Black Abbé; and what of him ? He is repenting to-night that he ever tried conclusions with me, I'll wager."

I spoke the more confidently because in my heart I was still troubled to know the meaning of the Abbé's glance.

" Hein," said Tamin. " He looked — his eyes would lift a scalp ! I was standing in the light just under the window, when of a sudden the door closed; and there he stood beside me, with no sound, and still as a heron. He looked at me with those two narrow eyes, as if he would eat my heart out; and I stood there, and shook. Then, of a sudden, his face changed. It became like a good priest's face when he says the prayer for the soul that is passing; and he looked at me with solemn eyes. And I was yet more afraid. 'It is not for me to rebuke you,' he said, speaking so that each word seemed an hour long; 'red runs your blood on the deep snow beneath the apple tree.' And before I could steady my teeth to ask him what he meant, he was gone. 'Red runs your blood beneath the apple tree.' What did he mean by that?"

"Oh," said I, speaking lightly to encourage him, though in truth the words fell on me with a chill, "he said it to spoil your sleep and poison your content. It was a cunning revenge, seeing that he dare not lift a hand to punish you otherwise."

"To be sure, my Tamin, that is all of it," added Marc. "Who has ever heard that the Black Abbé was a prophet? Faith, 'tis as Father says, a cunning and a devilish revenge. But you can balk it finely by paying no heed to it."

Tamin's face had brightened mightily, but he still looked serious.

"Do you think so?" he exclaimed with eagerness. "'Tis as you say indeed,—the Black Abbé is no prophet. Had it been Grûl, now, that said it, there were something to lie awake for, eh?"

"Yes, indeed, if Grûl had said it," muttered Marc, contemplating him strangely.

But for me, I was something impatient now to be asleep.

"Think no more of it, my friend," said I, and dismissed him. Yet sleepy as I was, I thought of it, and even I must have begun to dream of it. The white sheet of moonlight that lay across my couch became a drift of snow with blood upon it, and the patterned shadow upon the wall an apparition leaning over,— when out of an immense distance, as it were, I heard Marc's voice.

"Father," he cried softly, "are you awake?"

"Yes, dear lad," said I. "What is it?"

"I have been wondering," said he, "why the Black Abbé looked at you, not me, in his going. He had such a countenance as warns me that he purposes some cunning stroke. But I fear his enmity has turned from me to you."

"Well, lad, it was surely I that balked him. What would you have?" I asked.

"Oh," said he, heavily, "that I should have turned that bloodhound onto your trail!"

"Marc, if it will comfort you to know it, carry this in your memory," said I, with a cheerful lightness, like froth upon the strong emotion that flooded my heart. "When the Black Abbé strikes at me, it will be through you. He knows where I am like to prove most vulnerable!"

"'Tis all right, then, so as we sink or swim together, Father," said Marc, quietly.

"That's the way of it now, dear lad! Sweet sleep to you, and dreams of red hair!" said I. And I turned my face drowsily to the wall.

Chapter IX

The Abbé Strikes Again

THE few days of our stay at Chignecto were gay and busy ones; and all through them hummed the wind steadily across the pale green marshes, and buffeted the golden-rod on our high shoulder of upland. De Ramezay gratified me by making much of Marc. The three of us rode daily abroad among the surrounding settlements. And I spent many hours planning with de Ramezay a fort which should be built on the site of this camp, in case the coming campaign should fail to drive the English out of Acadie. De Ramezay, as was ever his wont, was full of confidence in the event. But of the sorry doings at Quebec, of the plundering hands upon the public purse, of the shamelessness in high places, he hinted to me so broadly that I began to see much ground for Marc's misgivings. And my heart cried out for my fair country of New France.

On the fifth day of our stay,—it was a Wednesday, and very early in the morning,—the good Beaudry with his good boat came for us. The tide serving at about two hours after sunrise, we set out then for Grand Pré, well content with the jade Fortune whose whims had so far favoured us. De Ramezay and his officers were at the wharf-end to bid us God-speed; and as I muse upon it now they may have thought curiously of it to see the loving fashion in which both Marc and I made a point to embrace our faithful Tamin. But that is neither here nor there, so long as we let him plainly understand how our hearts were towards him.

The voyage home was uneventful, save that we met contrary winds, whereby it fell that not until evening of the second day did we come into the Gaspereau mouth and mark the maids of Grand Pré carrying water from the village well.

The good Beaudry we paid to his satisfaction, and left to find lodging in one of the small houses by the water side; while Marc and I took our way up the long street with its white houses standing amid their apple trees. Having gone perhaps four or five furlongs, returning many a respectful salutation from the doorways as we passed, we then turned up the hill by a little lane which was bordered stiffly with the poplar trees of Lombardy, and in short space we came to a pleasant cottage in a garden, under shadow of the tall white church which stood sentinel over the Grand Pré roofs. The cottage had some apple trees behind it, and many late roses blooming in the garden. It was the home of the good Curé, Father Fafard, most faithful and most gentle of priests.

With Father Fafard we lodged that night, and for some days thereafter. The Curé's round face grew unwontedly stern and anxious as we told him our adventures, and rehearsed the doings of the Black Abbé. He got up from time to time and paced the room, muttering once—

"Alas that such a man should discredit our holy office! What wrath may he not bring down upon this land!"—and more to a like purport.

My own house in Grand Pré, where Marc had inhabited of late, and where I was wont to pay my flitting visits, I judged well to put off my hands for the present, foreseeing that troublous times were nigh. I transferred it in Father Fafard's presence to a trusty villager by name Marquette, whom I could count upon to transfer it back to me as soon as the skies should clear again. I knew that if, by any fortune of war, English troops should come to be quartered in Grand Pré, they would be careful for the property of the villagers; but the house and goods of an enemy under arms, such would belike fare ill. I collected, also, certain moneys due me in the village, for I knew that the people were prosperous, and I did not know how long their prosperity might continue. This done, Marc and I set out for my own estate beside the yellow Canard. There I had rents to gather in, but no house to put

off my hands.   At the time when Acadie
was ceded to England, a generation back,
the house of the de Mers had been handed
over to one of the most prosperous of our
habitants, and with that same family it had
ever since remained, yielding indeed a pre-
posterously scant rental, but untroubled
by the patient conqueror.

My immediate destination was the
Forge, where I expected to find Babin
awaiting me with news and messages.   At
the Forge, too, I would receive payment
from my tenants, and settle certain points
which, as I had heard, were at dispute
amongst them.

As we drew near the Forge, through the
pleasant autumn woods, it wanted about
an hour of noon.   I heard, far off, the
muffled thunder of a cock-partridge drum-
ming.   But there was no sound of hammer
on clanging anvil, no smoke rising from
the wide Forge chimney ; and when we
entered, the ashes were dead cold.   It was
plain there had been no fire in the forge
that day.

"Where can Babin be ? " I muttered in

vexation. "If he got my message, there can be no excuse for his absence."

"I'll wager, Father," said Marc, "that if he is not off on some errand of yours, then he is sick abed, or dead. Nought besides would keep Babin when you called him."

I went to a corner and pulled a square of bark from a seemingly hollow log up under the rafters. In the secret niche thus revealed was a scrap of birch bark scrawled with some rude characters of Babin's, whence I learned that my trusty smith was sick of a sharp inflammation. I passed the scrap over to Marc, and felt again in the hollow.

"What, in the name of all the saints, is this?" I exclaimed, drawing out a short piece of peeled stick. A portion of the stick was cut down to a flat surface, and on this was drawn with charcoal a straight line, having another straight line perpendicular to it, and bisecting it. At the top of the perpendicular was a figure of the sun, thus:—

"It's a message from Grûl," said Marc, the instant that his eyes fell upon it.

"H'm; and how do you know that?" said I, turning it over curiously in my fingers.

"Well," replied Marc, "the peeled stick is Grûl's sign manual. What does he say?"

"He seems to say that he is going to build a windmill," said I, with great seriousness; "but doubtless you will give this hieroglyphic quite a different interpretation."

Marc laughed, — yes, laughed audibly. And it is possible that his Penobscot grandmother turned in her grave. It was good to know that the lad *could* laugh, which I had begun to doubt; but it was puzzling to me to hear him laugh at the mere absurdity which I had just uttered, when my most polished witticisms, of which I had shot off many of late at Chignecto, and in conversation with good Father Fafard, had never availed to bring more than a phantom smile to his lips. However, I made no comment, but handed him "Grûl's sign manual," as he chose to call it.

"Why, Father," said he, "you understand it well enough, I know. This is plainly the sun at high noon. At high noon, therefore, we may surely expect to see Grûl. He has been here but a short time back; for see, the wood is not yet dry."

"Sapristi!" said I, "do you call that the sun, lad? It is very much like a windmill."

How Marc might have retorted upon me, I know not; for at the moment, though it yet wanted much of noon, the fantastic figure of the madman—if he were a madman—sped into the Forge. He stopped abruptly before us and scrutinized us for some few seconds in utter silence, his eyes glittering and piercing like sword points. His long white hair and beard were disordered with haste, the flowers and feathers in his pointed cap were for the most part broken, even as when we had last seen him, and his gaudy mantle was somewhat befouled with river mud. Yet such power was there in his look and in his gesture, that when he stretched out his little white staff toward me and said "Come," I had much ado to keep from obeying him without question. Yet this I would not permit myself, as was natural.

"Whither?" I questioned. "And for what purpose?"

By this time he was out at the door, but he stopped. Giving me a glance of scorn he turned to Marc, and stretched out his staff.

"Come," he said. And in a breath he was gone, springing with incredible swiftness and smoothness through the underbrush.

"We must follow, Father!" cried Marc; and in the same instant was away.

For my own part, it was sorely against me to be led by the nose, and thus blindly, by the madman—whom I now declared certainly to be mad. But Marc had gone, so I had no choice, as I conceived it, but to stand by the lad. I went too. And seeing that I had to do it, I did it well, and presently overtook them.

"What is this folly?" I asked angrily, panting a little, I confess.

But Marc signed to me to be silent. I obeyed, though with ill enough grace, and ran on till my mouth was like a board, my tongue like wool. Then the grim light of the forest whitened suddenly before us, and our guide stopped. Instinctively we imitated his motions, as he stole forward and peered through a screen of leafage. We were on a bank overlooking the Canard. A little below, and paddling swiftly towards the river-mouth, were two canoes manned with the Abbé's Micmacs. In the bottom of one canoe lay a little fair-haired boy, bound.

"My God!" cried Marc, under his breath, "'tis the child! 'tis little Philip Hanford."

Grûl turned his wild eyes upon us.

"The power of the dog!" he muttered, "the power of the dog!"

"We must get a canoe and follow them!" exclaimed Marc, in great agitation, turning to go, and looking at me with passionate appeal. But before I could speak, to assure him of my aid and support, Grûl interfered.

"Wait!" he said, with meaning emphasis, thrusting his little staff almost in the lad's face. "Come!" and he started up along the river bank, going swiftly but with noiseless caution. I expected Marc to demur, but not so. He evidently had a childlike faith in this fantastic being. He followed without a protest. Needless to say, I followed also. But all this mystery, and this blind obedience, and this lordly lack of explanation, were little to my liking.

We had not gone above half a mile when Grûl stopped, and bent his mad head to listen. Such an attitude of listening I had never seen before. The feathers and stalks in his cap seemed to lean forward like a horse's ears; his hair and beard took on a like inclination of intentness; even the grim little scarlet head upon his staff seemed to listen with its master. And Marc did as Grûl did. Then came a sound as of a woman weeping, very close at hand. Grûl motioned us to pass him, and creep forward. We did so, lying down and moving as softly as lizards. But I turned to see what our mysterious guide was doing — and lo, he was gone. He might have faded into a summer exhalation, so complete and silent was his exit.

This was too much. Only my experience as a woods-fighter, my instinctive caution, kept me from springing to my feet and calling him. But my suspicions were all on fire. I laid a firm hand of detention on Marc's arm, and whispered : —

" He's gone ; 'tis a trap."

Marc looked at me in some wonder, and more impatience.

" No trap, Father ; that's Grûl's way."

" Well," I whispered, " we had better go another way, I'm thinking."

As I spoke, the woman's weeping came to us more distinctly. Something in the sound seemed to catch Marc's heart, and his face changed.

" 'Tis all right, I tell you, Father ! "

came from between his teeth. "Come! come! Oh, I know the voice!" And he crept forward resolutely.

And, of course, I followed.

Chapter X

A Bit of White Petticoat

WE had not advanced above a score of paces when, peering stealthily between the stems of herbs and underbrush, we saw what Grûl had desired us to see. Two more canoes were drawn up at the water's edge. Four savages were in sight, sprawling in indolent attitudes under the shade of a wide water-maple. In their midst, at the foot of the tree, lay a woman bound securely. She was huddled together in a posture of hopeless despair; and a dishevelled glory of gold-red tresses fell over her face to hide it. She lay in a moveless silence. Yet the sound of weeping continued, and Marc, gripping my hand fiercely, set his mouth to my ear and gasped : —

"'Tis my own maid! 'Tis Prudence!"

Then I saw where she sat, a little apart, a slender maid with a lily face, and hair glowing dark red in the full sun that streamed upon her. She was so tied to another tree that she might have no comfort or companionship of her sister, — for I needed now no telling to convey it to me that the lady with the hidden face and the unweeping anguish was Mistress Mizpah Hanford, mother of the child whom I had just seen carried away.

I grieved for Marc, whose eyes stared out upon the weeping maid from a face that had fallen to the hue of ashes. But I praised the saints for sending to our aid this madman Grûl, — whom, in my heart, I now graciously absolved from the charge of madness. Seeing the Black Abbé's hand in the ravishment of these tender victims, I made no doubt to cross him yet again, and my heart rose exultantly to the enterprise.

"Cheer up, lad," I whispered to Marc. "Come away a little till we plot."

I showed my confidence in my face, and I could see that he straightway took heart

thereat.   Falling back softly for a space
of several rods, we paused in a thicket to
take counsel.   As soon as we could speak
freely, Marc exclaimed, " They may go at
any moment, Father.   We must haste."

" No," said I, " they'll not go till the
cool of the day.   The others went because
they have plainly been ordered to part the
child from his mother.   It is a most cunning and most cruel malice that could so
order it."

" It is my enemy's thrust at me," said
Marc.   " How did he know that I loved
the maid ? "

" His eyes are in every corner of Acadie," said I ; " but we will foil him in this
as in other matters.   Marc, my heart is
stirred mightily by that poor mother's
pain.   I tell you, lad," — and I looked
diligently to the priming of my pistols as
I spoke, — " I tell you I will not rest till
I give the little one back into her arms."

But Marc, as was not unnatural, thought
now rather of his lily maid sobbing under
the tree.

" Yes, Father," said he, " but what is

to be done now, to save Prudence and Mizpah?"

"Of course, dear lad," I answered, smilingly, "that is just what we are here for. But let me consider." And sitting down upon a fallen tree, I buried my face in my hands. Marc, the while, waited with what patience he could muster, relying wholly upon my conduct of the business, but fretting for instant action.

We were well armed (each with a brace of pistols and a broadsword, the forest being no place for rapiers), and I accounted that we were an overmatch for the four redskins. But there was much at stake, with always the chance of accident. And, moreover, these Indians were allies of France, wherefore I was most unwilling to attack them from the advantage of an ambush. These various considerations decided me.

"Marc, we'll fight them if needful," said I, lifting up my head. "But I'm going to try first the conclusions of peace. I will endeavour to ransom the prisoners. These Micmacs are mightily avaricious, and may yield. It goes against me to attack them from an ambush, seeing that they are of our party and servants of King Louis."

At this speech Marc looked very ill content.

" But, Father," he objected, " shall we forego the advantage of a surprise? We are but two to their four, and we put the whole issue at hazard. And as for their being of our party, they bring shame upon our party, and greatly dishonour the service of King Louis."

" Nevertheless, dear lad," said I, " they have their claim upon us, — not lightly to be overlooked, in my view of it. But hear my plan. You will go back to where we lay a moment ago, and there be ready with your pistols. I will approach openly by the water side and enter into parley with them. If I can buy the captives, well and good. If they deny me, we quarrel. You will know when to play your part. I am satisfied of that. I shall feel safe under cover of your pistols, and shall depend upon you to account for two of the four. Only, do not be too hasty!"

"Oh, I'm cool as steel now, Father," said Marc. "But I like not this plan. The danger is all yours. And the quarrel is mine. Let us go into it side by side!"

"Chut, lad!" said I. "Your quarrel's my quarrel, and the danger is not more for me than for you, as you won't be long away from me when the fight begins, — if it comes to a fight. And further, my plan is both an honest one and like to succeed. Come, let us be doing!"

Marc seized my hand, and gave me a look of pride and love which put a glow at my heart. "You know best, Father," said he. And turning away, he crept toward his post. For me, I made a circuit, in leisurely fashion, and came out upon the shore behind a point some rods below the spot where the savages lay. Then I walked boldly up along the water's edge.

The Indians heard me before I came in view, and were on their feet when I appeared around the point. They regarded me with black suspicion, but no hostile movement, as I strode straight up to them and greeted, fairly enough but coldly, a tall warrior, whom I knew to be one of the Black Abbé's lieutenants. He grunted, and asked me who I was.

"You know well enough who I am," said I, seating myself carelessly upon a rock, "seeing that you had a chief hand in the outrages put upon me the other day by that rascally priest of yours!"

At this the chief stepped up to me with an air of menace, his high-cheeked, coppery face scowling with wrath. But I eyed him steadily, and raised my hand with a little gesture of authority. "Wait!" said I; and he paused doubtfully. "I have no grudge against you for that," I went on. "You but obeyed your master's orders faithfully, as you will doubtless obey mine a few weeks hence, when I take command of your rabble and try to make you of some real service to the King. I am one of the King's captains."

At this the savage looked puzzled,

while his fellows grunted in manifest uncertainty.

" What you want ? " he asked bluntly.

I looked at him for some moments without replying. Then I glanced at the form of Mizpah Hanford, still unmoving, the face still hidden under that pathetic splendour of loosened hair. Prudence I could not catch view of, by reason of another tree which intervened. But the sound of her weeping had ceased.

" I am ready to ransom these prisoners of yours," said I.

The savages glanced furtively at each other, but the coppery masks of their features betrayed nothing.

" Not for ransom," said the chief, with a dogged emphasis.

I opened my eyes wide. " You astonish me ! " said I. " Then how will they profit you ? If you wanted their scalps, those you might have taken at Annapolis."

At that word, revealing that I knew whence they came, I took note of a stir in the silent figure beneath the maple. I felt that her eyes were watching me from behind that sumptuous veil which her bound hands could not put aside. I went on, with a sudden sense of exaltation.

"Give me these prisoners," I urged, half pleading, half commanding. "They are useless to you except for ransom. I will give you more than any one else will give you. Tell me your price."

But the savage was obstinate.

"Not for ransom," he repeated, shaking his head.

"You are afraid of your priest," said I, with slow scorn. "He has told you to bring them to him. And what will you get? A pistole or two for each! But I will give you gold, good French crowns, ten times as much as you ever got before!"

As I spoke, one of the listening savages got up, his eyes a-sparkle with eagerness, and muttered something in Micmac, which I could not understand. But the chief turned upon him so angrily that he slunk back, abashed.

"Agree with me now," I said earnestly. "Then wait here till I fetch the gold, and

I will deliver it into your hands before you deliver the captives."

But the chief merely turned aside with an air of settling the question, and repeated angrily : —

" I say white girls not for ransom."

I rose to my feet.

" Fools, you are," said I, "and no men, but sick women, afraid of your rascal priest. I offered to buy when I might have taken ! Now I will take, and you will get no ransom ! Unloose their bonds ! "

And I pointed with my sword, while my left hand rested upon a pistol in my belt. I am a very pretty shot with my left hand.

Before the words were fairly out of my lips the four sprang at me. Stepping lightly aside, I fired the pistol full at the chief's breast, and he plunged headlong. In the next instant came a report from the edge of the underbrush, and a second savage staggered, groaned, and fell upon his knees, while Marc leaped down and rushed upon a third. The remaining one snatched up his musket (the muskets were forgotten at the first, when I seemed to be alone), and took a hasty aim at me; but before he could pull the trigger my second pistol blazed in his face, and he dropped, while his weapon, exploding harmlessly, knocked up some mud and grass. I saw Marc chase his antagonist to the canoes at the point of his sword, and prick him lightly for the more speed. But at the same instant, out of the corner of my eye, I saw the savage whom Marc's shot had brought down struggle again to his feet and swing his hatchet. With a yell I was upon him, and my sword point (the point is swifter than the edge in an emergency) went through his throat with a sobbing click. But I was just too late. The hatchet had left his hand; and the flying blade caught Marc in the shoulder. The sword dropped from his grasp, he reeled, and sat down with a shudder before I could get to his side. I paid no further heed to the remaining Indian, but was dimly conscious of him launching a canoe and paddling away in wild haste.

I lifted the dear lad into the shade, and anxiously examined the wound.

" 'Tis but a flesh wound," said he, faintly ; but I found that the blow had not only grievously gashed the flesh, but split the shoulder blade.

" Flesh wound ! " I muttered. " You'll do no more fighting in this campaign, dear lad, unless they put it off till next spring. This shoulder will be months in mending."

" When it does mend, will my arm be the same as ever ? " he asked, somewhat tremulously. " 'Tis my sword arm."

" Yes, lad, yes ; you need not trouble about that," said I. " But it is a case for care."

In the meantime, I was cleansing the wound with salt water which I had brought from the river in my cap. Now, I cast about in my mind for a bandage ; and I looked at the prisoner beneath the maple. Marc first, courtesy afterwards, I thought in my heart ; for I durst not leave the wound exposed with so many flies in the air.

The lady's little feet, bound cruelly,

were drawn up in part beneath her dark skirt, but so that a strip of linen petticoat shone under them. I hesitated, but only for a second. Lifting the poor little feet softly to one side, with a stammered, "Your pardon, Madame, but the need is instant!" I slit off a breadth of the soft white stuff with my sword. And I was astonished to feel my face flush hotly as I did it. With strangely thrilling fingers, and the help of my sword edge, I then set free her feet, and with no more words turned hastily back to Marc, abashed as a boy.

In a few moments I had Marc's wound softly dressed, for I had some skill in this rough and ready surgery. I could see by his contracting pupils that the hurt was beginning to agonize, but the dear lad never winced under my fingers, and I commended him heartily as a brave patient. Then placing a bundle of cool ferns under his head for a pillow, I turned to the captives, from whom there had been never a word this while.

Chapter XI

I Fall a Willing Captive

THE lady whose feet I had freed had risen so far as to rest crouching against the gnarled trunk of the maple tree. The glorious abundance of her hair she had shaken back, revealing a white face chiselled like a Madonna's, a mouth somewhat large, with lips curved passionately, and great sea-coloured eyes which gazed upon me from dark circles of pain. But the face was drawn now with that wordless and tearless anguish which makes all utterance seem futile, —the anguish of a mother whose child has been torn from her arms and carried she knows not whither. Her hands lay in her lap, tight bound; and I noted their long, white slenderness. I felt as if I should go on my knees to serve her — I who had but just now served her with such scant courtesy as it shamed my soul to think on. As I bent low to loose her hands, I sought in my mind for phrases of apology that might show at the same time my necessity and my contrition. But lifting my eyes for an instant to hers, I was pierced with a sense of the anguish which was rending her heart, and straightway I forgot all nice phrases.

What I said — the words coming from my lips abruptly — was this: "I will find him! I will save him! Be comforted, Madame! He shall be restored to you!"

In great, simple matters, how little explanation seems needed. She asked not who I was, how I knew, whom I would save, how it was to be done; and I thrill proudly even now to think how my mere word convinced her. The tense lines of her face yielded suddenly, and she broke into a shaking storm of tears, moaning faintly over and over — "Philip! — Oh, my Philip! — Oh, my boy!" I watched her with a great compassion. Then, ere I could prevent, she amazed me by snatching my hand and pressing it to her lips. But she spoke no word of thanks. Drawing my hand gently away, in great embarrassment, I repeated: "Believe me, oh, believe me, Madame; I *will* save the little one." Then I went to release the other captive, whom I had well-nigh forgotten the while.

This lily maid of Marc's, this Prudence, I found in a white tremour of amazement and inquiry. From where she sat in her bonds, made fast to her tree, she could see nothing of what went on, but she could hear everything, and knew she had been rescued. It was a fair, frank, childlike face she raised to mine as I smiled down upon her, swiftly and gently severing her bonds; and I laid a hand softly on that rich hair which Marc had praised, being right glad he loved so sweet a maid as this. I forgot that I must have seemed to her in this act a shade familiar, my fatherly forty years not showing in my face. So, indeed, it was for an instant, I think ; for she coloured maidenly. But seeing the great kindness in my eyes, the thought was gone. Her own eyes filled with tears, and she sprang up and clung to me, sobbing, like a child just awakened in the night from a bad dream.

"Oh," she panted, "are they gone? did you kill them? how good you are! Oh, God will reward you for being so good to us!" And she trembled so she would certainly have fallen if I had not held her close.

"You are safe now, dear," said I, soothing her, quite forgetting that she knew me not as I knew her, and that, if she gave the matter any heed at all, my speech must have puzzled her sorely. "But come with me!" And I led her to where Marc lay in the shade.

The dear lad's face had gone even whiter than when I left him, and I saw that he had swooned.

"The pain and shock have overcome him!" I exclaimed, dropping on my knees to remove the pillow of ferns from under his head. As I did so, I heard the girl catch her breath sharply, with a sort of moan, and glancing up, I saw her face all drawn with misery. While I looked in some surprise, she suddenly threw herself down, and crushed his face in her bosom, quite shutting off the air, which he, being in a faint, greatly needed. I was about to protest, when her words stopped me.

"Marc, Marc," she moaned, "why did you betray us? Oh, why did you betray us so cruelly? But oh, I love you even if you *were* a traitor. Now you are dead" (she had not heard me, evidently, saying he had swooned), "now you are dead I may love you, no matter what you did. Oh, my love, why did you, why did you?" And while I listened in bewilderment, she sprang to her feet, and her blue eyes blazed upon me fiercely.

"You killed him!" she hissed at me across his body.

This I remembered afterwards. At the moment I only knew that she was calling the lad a traitor. That I was well tired of.

"Madame!" said I, sternly. "Do not presume so far as to touch him again."

It was her turn to look astonished now. Her eyes faltered from my angry face to Marc's, and back again in a kind of helplessness.

"Oh, you do well to accuse him," I went on, bitterly, — perhaps not very relevantly. "You shall not dishonour him by touching him, you, who can believe vile lies of the loyal gentleman who loves you, and has, it may be, given his life for the girl who now insults him."

The girl's face was now in such a confusion of distress that I almost, but not quite, pitied her. Ere she could find words to reply, however, her sister was at her side, catching her hands, murmuring at her ear.

"Why, Prudence, child," she said, "don't you see it all? Didn't you see it all? How splendidly Marc saved us" (I blessed the tact which led her to put the first credit on Marc) — "Marc and this most brave and gallant gentleman? It was one of the savages who struck

Marc down, before my eyes, as he was fighting to save us. That dreadful story was a lie, Prudence; don't you see?"

The maid saw clearly enough, and with a mighty gladness. She was for throwing herself down again beside the lad to cover his face with kisses — and shut off the air which he so needed. But I thrust her aside. She had believed Marc a traitor. Marc might forgive her when he could think for himself. I was in no mind to.

She looked at me with unutterable reproach, her eyes filling and running over, but she drew back submissively.

" I know," she said, " I don't deserve that you should let me go near him. But — I think — I think he would want me to, sir! See, he wants me! Oh, let me!" And I perceived that Marc's eyes had opened. They saw no one but the maid, and his left hand reached out to her.

" Oh, well!" said I, grimly. And thereafter it seemed to me that the lad got on with less air than men are accustomed to need when they would make recovery from a swoon.

I turned to Mizpah Hanford; and I wondered what sort of eyes were in Marc's head, that he should see Prudence when Mizpah was by. Before I could speak, Mizpah began to make excuses for her sister. With heroic fortitude she choked back her own grief, and controlled her voice with a brave simplicity. Coming from her lips, these broken excuses seemed sufficient — though to this day I question whether I ought to have relented so readily. She pleaded, and I listened, and was content to listen so long as she would continue to plead. But there was little I clearly remember. At last, however, these words, with which she concluded, aroused me : —

"How could we any longer refuse to believe," she urged, "when the good priest confessed to us plainly, after much questioning, that it was Monsieur Marc de Mer who had sent the savages to steal us, and had told them just the place to find us, and the hour? The savages had told us the same thing at first, taunting us with it when we threatened them with

Marc's vengeance. You see, Monsieur, they had plainly been informed by some one of our little retreat at the riverside, and of the hour at which we were wont to frequent it. Yet we repudiated the tale with horror. Then yesterday, when the good priest told us the same thing, with a reluctance which showed his horror of it, what *could* we do but believe? Though it did seem to us that if Marc were false there could be no one true. The priest believed it. He was kind and pitiful, and tried to get the savages to set us free. He talked most earnestly, most vehemently to them; but it was in their own barbarous language, and of course we could not understand. He told us at last that he could do nothing at the time, but that he would exert himself to the utmost to get us out of their hands by and by. Then he went away. And then —"

"And then, Madame," said I, "your little one was taken from you at his orders!"

"Why, what do you mean, Monsieur?" she gasped, her great sea-coloured

eyes opening wide with fresh terror. "At
his orders? By the orders of that kind
priest?"

"Of what appearance was he?" I inquired, in return.

"Oh," she cried breathlessly, "he was
square yet spare of figure, dark-skinned
almost as Marc, with a very wide lower
face, thin, thin lips, and remarkably light
eyes set close together, — a strange, strong
face that might look very cruel if he were
angry. He looked angry once when he
was arguing with the Indians."

"You have excellently described our
bitterest foe, and yours, Madame," said I,
smiling. "The wicked Abbé La Garne,
the pastor and master of these poor tools
of his whom I would fain have spared,
but could not." And I pointed to the
bodies of the three dead savages, where
they lay sprawling in various pathetic
awkwardnesses of posture.

She looked, seemed to think of them
for the first time, shivered, and turned
away her pitiful eyes.

"Those poor wretches," I continued,

"were sent by this kind priest to capture you. He knew when and where to find you, because he had played the eavesdropper when Marc and I were talking of you."

"Oh," she cried, clenching her white hands desperately, "can there be a priest so vile?"

"Ay, and this which you have heard is but a part of his villany. We have but lately baulked him in a plot whereby he had nearly got Marc hanged. This, Madame, I promise myself the honour of relating to you by and by; but now we must get the poor lad removed to some sort of house and comfort."

"And, oh," cried this poor mother, in a voice of piercing anguish and amazement, as if she could not yet wholly realize it, — "my boy, my boy! He is in the power of such a monster!"

"Be of good heart, I beseech you," said I, with a kind of passion in my voice. "I will find him, I swear I will bring him back to you. I will wait only so long as to see my own boy in safe hands!"

Again that look of trust was turned upon me, thrilling me with invincible resolve.

"Oh, I trust you, Monsieur!" she cried.   Then pressing both hands to her eyes with a pathetic gesture, and thrusting back her hair — "I knew you, somehow, for the Seigneur de Briart," she went on, "as soon as I heard you demanding our release.   And I immediately felt a great hope that you would set us free and save Philip.   I suppose it is from Marc that I have learned such confidence, Monsieur!"

I bowed, awkward and glad, and without a pretty word to repay her with, — I who have some name in Quebec for well-turned compliment.   But before this woman, who was young enough to be my daughter, I was like a green boy.

"You are too kind," I stammered.   "It will be my great ambition to justify your good opinion of me."

Then I turned away to launch a canoe.

While I busied myself getting the canoe ready, and spreading ferns in the bottom of it for Marc to lie on, Mizpah walked up and down in a kind of violent speechlessness, as it were, twisting her long white hands, but no more giving voice to her grief and her anxiety. Once she sat down abruptly under the maple tree, and buried her face in her hands. Her shoulders shook, but not a sound of sob or moan came to my ears. My heart ached at the sight. I determined that I would give her work to do, such as would compel some attention on her part.

As soon as the canoe was ready I asked :

" Can you paddle, Madame ? "

She nodded an affirmative, her voice seeming to have gone from her.

" Very well," said I, " then you will take the bow paddle, will you not ? "

" Yes, indeed ! " she found voice to cry, with an eagerness which I took to signify that she thought by paddling hard to find her child the sooner. But the manner in which she picked up the paddle, and took her place, and held the canoe, showed me she was no novice in the art of canoeing.

I now went to lift Marc and carry him to the canoe.

" Let me help you," pleaded Prudence, springing up from beside him.   " He must be so heavy !"   Whereat I laughed.

" I can walk, I am sure, Father," said Marc, faintly, " if you put me on my feet and steady me."

" I doubt it, lad," said I, " and 'tis hardly worth while wasting your little strength in the attempt. Now, Prudence," I went on, turning to the girl, " I want you to get in there in front of the middle bar, and make a comfortable place for this man's head, — if you don't mind taking a *live* traitor's head in your lap ! "

At this the poor girl's face flushed scarlet, as she quickly seated herself in the canoe ; and her lips trembled so that my heart smote me for the jest.

" Forgive me, child. I meant it not as a taunt, but merely as a poor jest," I hastened to explain. " Your sister has told me all, and you were scarce to blame. Now, take the lad and make him as comfortable as a man with a shattered shoulder can hope to be." And I laid Marc gently down so that he could slip his long legs under the bar.   He straightway closed his eyes from sheer weakness ; but he could feel his maid bend her blushing face over his, and his expression was a strangely mingled one of suffering and content.

Taking my place in the stern of the canoe, I pushed out.   The tide was just beginning to ebb.   There was no wind. The shores were green and fair on either hand.   My dear lad, though sore hurt, was happy in the sweet tenderness of his lily maid.   As for me, I looked perhaps overmuch at the radiant head of Mizpah, at the lithe vigorous swaying of her long arms, the play of her gracious shoulders as she paddled strenuously.   I felt that it was good to be in this canoe, all of us together, floating softly down to the little village beside the Canard's mouth.

Part II

Mizpah

Chapter XII

In a Strange Fellowship

I TOOK Marc and the ladies to the house of one Giraud, a well-tried and trusted retainer, to whom I told the whole affair. Then I sent a speedy messenger to Father Fafard, begging him to come at once. The Curé of Grand Pré was a skilled physician, and I looked to him to treat Marc's wound better than I could hope to do. My purpose, as I unfolded it to Marc and to the ladies that same evening, sitting by Marc's pallet at the open cottage door, was to start the very next day in quest of the stolen child. I would take but one follower, to help me paddle, for I would rely not on force but on cunning in this venture. I would warn some good men among my tenants, and certain others who were in the coun-

sels of the Forge, to keep an unobtrusive
guard about the place, till Marc's wound
should be so far healed that he might go
to Grand Pré.   And further, I would put
them all in the hands of Father Fafard,
with whom even the Black Abbé would
scarce dare to meddle openly.

"The Curé," said I, turning to Mizpah,
"you may trust both for his wisdom and
his goodness.   With him you will all be
secure till my return."

Mizpah bowed her head in acknowl-
edgment, and looked at me gratefully,
but could not trust herself to speak.
She sat a little apart, by the door, and
was making a mighty effort to maintain
her outward composure.

Then I turned to where Marc's face,
pallid but glad, shone dimly on his pillow.
I took his hand, I felt his pulse — for the
hundredth time, perhaps.   There was no
more fever, no more prostration, than was
to be accounted inevitable from such a
wound.   So I said : —

" Does the plan commend itself to you,
dear lad ?   It troubles me sore to leave

you in this plight; but Father Fafard is skilful, and I think you will not fret for lack of tender nursing. You will not *need* me, lad; but there is a little lad with yellow hair who needs me now, and I must go to him."

The moment I had spoken these last words I wished them back, for Mizpah broke down all at once in a terrible passion of tears. But I was ever a bungler where women are concerned, ever saying the wrong thing, ever slow to understand their strange, swift shiftings of mood. This time, however, I understood; for with my words a black realization of the little one's lonely fear came down upon my own soul, till my heart cried out with pity for him; and Prudence fell a-weeping by Marc's head. But she stopped on the instant, fearing to excite Marc hurtfully, and Marc said : —

" Indeed, Father, think not a moment more of me. 'Tis the poor little lad that needs you. Oh that I too could go with you on the quest ! "

" 'To-morrow I go," said I, positively,

"just as soon as I have seen Father Fafard."

As I spoke, Mizpah went out suddenly, and walked with rapid strides down the road, passing Giraud on the way as he came from mending the little canoe which I was to take. I had chosen a small and light craft, not knowing what streams I might have to ascend, what long carries I might have to make. As Mizpah passed him, going on to lean her arms upon the fence and stare out across the water, Giraud turned to watch her for a moment. Then, as he came up to the door where we sat, he took off his woollen cap, and said simply, "Poor lady! it goes hard with her."

"My friend," said I, "will these, while I am gone, be safe here from their enemies, — even should the Black Abbé come in person?"

"Master," he replied, with a certain proud nobility, which had ever impressed me in the man, "if any hurt comes to them, it will be not over my dead body alone, but over those of a dozen more stout fellows who would die to serve you."

" I believe you," said I, reaching out my hand. He kissed it, and went off quickly about his affairs.

Hardly was he gone when Mizpah came back. She was very pale and calm, and her eyes shone with the fire of some intense purpose. Had I known woman's heart as do some of my friends whom I could mention, I should have fathomed that purpose at her first words. But as I have said, I am slow to understand a woman's hints and objects, though men I can read ere their thoughts find speech. There was a faint glory of the last of sunset on Mizpah's face and hair as she stood facing me, her lips parted to speak. Behind her lay the little garden, with its sunflowers and lupines, and its thicket of pole beans in one corner. Then, beyond the gray fence, the smooth tide of the expanding river, violet-hued, the copper and olive wood, the marshes all greenish amber, and the dusky purple of the hills. It was all stamped upon my memory in delectable and imperishable colours, though I know that at the moment I saw only Mizpah's tall grace, her red-gold hair, the eyes that seemed to bring my spirit to her feet. I was thinking, "Was there ever such another woman's face, or a presence so gracious?" when I realized that she was speaking.

"Do I paddle well, Monsieur?" she asked, with the air of one who repeats a question.

"Pardon, a thousand pardons, Madame!" I exclaimed. "Yes, you use your paddle excellently well."

"And I can shoot, I can shoot very skilfully," she went on, with strong emphasis. "I can handle both pistol and musket."

"Indeed, Madame!" said I, considerably astonished.

"Ask Marc if I am not a cunning shot," she persisted, while her eyes seemed to burn through me in their eager intentness.

"Yes, Father," came Marc's whispered response out of the shadow, where I saw only the bended head of the maid Prudence. "Yes, Father, she is a more cunning marksman than I."

I turned again to her, and saw that she expected, that she thirsted for, an answer. But what answer?

" Madame," said I, bowing profoundly, and hoping to cover my bewilderment with a courtly speech, " may I hope that you will fire a good shot for me some day; I should account it an honour above all others if I might be indebted to such a hand for such succour."

She clasped her hands in a great gladness, crying, "Then I *may* go with you?"

"Go with me!" I cried, looking at her in huge amazement.

"She wants to help you find the child," whispered Marc.

The thought of this white girl among the perils which I saw before me pierced my heart with a strange pang, and in my haste I cried rudely : —

"Nonsense! Impossible! Why, it would be mere madness!"

So bitter was the pain of disappointment which wrung her face that I put
out both hands towards her in passionate
deprecation.

"Forgive me; oh, forgive me, Madame!" I pleaded. "But how *could* I
bring you into such perils?"

But she caught my hands and would
have gone on her knees to me if I had
not stayed her roughly.

"Take me with you," she implored.
"I can paddle, I can serve you as well
as any man whom you can get. And I
am brave, believe me. And how *can* I
wait here when my boy, my darling, my
Philip, is alone among those beasts? I
would die every hour."

How could I refuse her? Yet refuse
her I would, I must. To take her would
be to lessen my own powers, I thought,
and to add tenfold to the peril of the
venture. Nevertheless my heart did now
so leap at the thought of this strange,
close fellowship which she demanded,
that I came near to silencing my better
judgment, and saying she might go.

But I shut my teeth obstinately on the words.

At this moment, while she waited trembling, Marc once more intervened.

"You might do far worse than take her, Father. No one else will serve you more bravely or more skilfully, I think."

So Marc actually approved of this incredible proposal? Then was it, after all, so preposterous? My wavering must have shown itself in my face, for her own began to lighten rarely.

"But—those clothes!" said I.

At this she flushed to her ears. But she answered bravely.

"I will wear others; did you think I would so hamper you with this guise? No," she added with a little nervous laugh, "I will play the man; be sure."

And so, though I could scarce believe it, it was settled that Mizpah Hanford should go with me.

That night I found little sleep. My thoughts were a chaos of astonishment and apprehension. Marc, moreover, kept tossing, for his wound fretted him sorely, and I was continually at his side to give him drink. At about two in the morning there came a horseman to the garden gate, riding swiftly. Hurrying out I met him in the path. It was Father Fafard, come straight upon my word. He turned his horse into Giraud's pasture, put saddle and bridle in the porchway, and then followed me in to Marc's bedside.

When he had dressed the wound anew, and administered a soothing draught, Marc fell into a quiet sleep.

"He will do well, but it is a matter for long patience," said the Curé.

Then we went out of the house and down to the garden corner by the thicket of beans, where we might talk freely and jar no slumberers. Father Fafard fell in with my plans most heartily, and accepted my charges. To hold the Black Abbé in check at any point, would, he felt, be counted unto him for righteousness.

My mind being thus set at ease, I resolved to start as soon as might be after daybreak.

Before it was yet full day, I was again

astir, and goodwife Giraud was getting ready, in bags, our provision of bacon and black bread. I had many small things to do, — gathering ammunition for two muskets and four pistols, selecting my paddles with care from Giraud's stock, and loading the canoe to the utmost advantage for ease of running and economy of space. Then, as I went in to the goodwife's breakfast, I was met at the door by a slim youth in leathern coat and leggins, with two pistols and Marc's whinger. I recognized the carven hilt stuck bravely in his belt, and Marc's knitted cap of gray wool on his head, well pulled down. The boy blushed, but met my eye with a sweet firmness, and I bowed with great courtesy. Even in this attire I thought she could not look aught but womanly — for it was Mistress Mizpah. Yet I could not but confess that to the stranger she would appear but as a singularly handsome stripling. The glory of her hair was hidden within her cap.

"These are the times," said I, seriously, "that breed brave women."

Breakfast done, messages and orders

repeated, and farewells all spoken, the sun was perhaps an hour high when we paddled away from the little landing under Giraud's garden fence. I waved my cap backwards to Prudence and the Curé, where they stood side by side at the landing. My comrade in the bow waved her hand once, then fell to paddling diligently. I was still in a maze of wonderment, ready at any time to wake and find it a dream. But the little seas that slapped us as we cleared the river mouth, these were plainly real. I headed for the eastern point of the island, intending to land at the mouth of the Piziquid and make some inquiries. The morning air was like wine in my veins. There was a gay dancing of ripples over toward Blomidon, and the sky was a clear blue. A dash of cool drops wet me. It was no dream.

And so in a strange fellowship I set out to find the child.

Chapter XIII

My Comrade

I COULD not sufficiently commend the ease and aptness with which my beautiful comrade wielded her paddle. But in a while the day grew hot, and I bade her lie back in her place and rest. At first she would not, till I was compelled to remind her in a tone of railing that I was the captain in this enterprise, and that good soldiers must obey. Whereupon, though her back was toward me, I saw a flush creep around to her little ears, and she laid the paddle down something abruptly. I feared that I had vexed her, and I made haste to attempt an explanation, although it seemed to me that she should have understood a matter so obvious.

"I beg you to pardon me, Madame,

if I seem to insist too much," said I, with hesitation. "But you must know that, if you exhaust yourself at the beginning of the journey, before you are hardened to the long continuance of such work, you will be unable to do anything to-morrow, and our quest will be much hindered."

"Forgive me!" she cried; "you are right, of course. Oh, I fear I have done wrong in hampering you! But I am strong, truly, and enduring as most men, Monsieur."

"Yes," I answered, "but to do one thing strenuously all day long, and for days thereafter, that is hard. I believe you can do it, or I should have been mad indeed to bring you. But you must let me advise you at the beginning. For this first day, rest often and save yourself as much as possible. By this means you will be able to do better to-morrow, and better still the day after. By the other means, you will be able to do little to-morrow most likely, and perhaps nothing the day after."

"Well," she said, turning her head partly around, so that I could see the gracious profile, "tell me, Monsieur, when to work and when to rest. I will obey. It is a lucky soldier, I know, who has the Seigneur de Briart to command him."

"But I fear, Madame," said I, "that discipline would sadly suffer if he had often such soldiers to command."

To this she made no reply. I saw that she leaned back in her place and changed her posture, so as to fulfil my wish and rest herself to the best advantage. I thought my words over. To me they seemed to have that savour of compliment which I would now avoid. I felt that here, under these strange circumstances, in an intimacy which might by and by be remembered by her with some little confusion, but which now, while she had no thought but for the rescue of the little one, contained no shadow of awkwardness for her clear and earnest soul, — I felt that here I must hold myself under bonds. The play of graceful compliment, such as I would have practised in her drawing-room to show her the courtliness of my breeding, must be forsworn. The admiration, the devotion, the worship, that burned in my eyes whensoever they dwelt upon her, must be strictly veiled. I must seem to forget that I am a man and my companion the fairest of women. Yes, I kept telling myself, I must regard her as a comrade only, and a follower, and a boy. I must be frank and careless in my manner toward her; kind, but blunt and positive. She will think nothing of it now, and will blush the less for it by and by, when the child is in her arms again, and she can once more give her mind to little matters.

And so I schooled myself; and as I watched her I began to realize more and more, with a delicious warming of my heart, what instant need I had of such schooling if I would not have her see how I was not at all her captain, but her bondsman.

At the mouth of the Piziquid stream

there clustered a few cottages, not enough
to call a village; and here we stopped
about noon. A meal of milk and eggs
and freshly baked rye cakes refreshed us,
and eager as was our haste, I judged it
wise to rest an hour stretched out in the
shade of an apple tree. To this halt,
Mizpah, after one glance of eager question at my face, made no demur, and I
replied to the glance by whispering:—

"That is a good soldier! We will gain
by this pause, now. We will travel late
to-night."

The cottagers of whom we had our
meal were folk unknown to me; and
being informed that the Black Abbé had
some followers in the neighbourhood, I
durst give no hint of our purpose. By
and by I asked carelessly if two canoes,
with Indians of the Shubenacadie, had
gone by this way. I thought that the
man looked at me with some suspicion.
He hesitated. But before he could reply
his goodwife answered for him, with the
freedom of a clear conscience.

"Yes, M'sieu," she chattered, "two

canoes, and four Indians. They went by yesterday, toward sundown, stopping here for water from our well,— the finest water hereabouts, if I do say it!"

"They went up the river, I suppose," said I.

"Oh, but no, M'sieu," clattered on the worthy dame. "They went straight up the bay. Yes, goodman," she continued, changing her tone sharply, "whenever I open my mouth you glare at me as if I was talking nonsense. What have I said wrong now, I'd like to know. Yes, I'd like very much to know that, goodman. Why should not the gentleman know that they had—"

But here the man interrupted her roughly. "Will you never be done your prating?" he cried. "Can't you see that you worry the gentlemen? How should they care to know that the red rascals made a good catch of shad off the island? Now, do go and get some of your fresh buttermilk for the gentlemen to drink before they go. Don't you see they are starting?"

And, indeed, Mizpah's impatience to be gone was plainly evident, and we had rested long enough. I durst not look at her face, lest our host should perceive that I had heard what I wanted to hear. I spoke casually of the weather, and inquired how his apples and his flax were faring, and so filled the minutes safely until the goodwife came with the buttermilk. Having both drunk gratefully of the cool, delicately acid, nourishing liquor, we gave the man a piece of silver, and set out in good heart.

"We are on the right track, comrade," said I, lightly, steering my course along the shore toward Cobequid.

Her only answer was to fall a-paddling with such an eagerness that I had to check her.

"Now, now," I said, "more haste, less speed."

"But I feel so strong now, and so rested," she cried passionately. "Might we not overtake them to-night?"

"Hardly so soon as that, I fear, Madame," I answered. "This is a stern chase, and it is like to be a long one; you must make up your mind to that, if you would not have a fresh disappointment every hour."

"Oh," she broke out, "if it were *your* child you were trying to find and save, you would not be so cool about it."

"Believe me, Madame," said I, in a low voice, "I am not perhaps as cool as I appear."

"Oh, what a weak and silly creature I must seem to you!" she cried. "But I will not be weak and silly when it comes to trial, Monsieur, I promise you. I *will* prove worthy of your confidence. But make allowance for me now, and do not judge me harshly. Every moment I seem to hear him crying for me, Monsieur." And her head drooped forward in unspeakable grief.

I could think of nothing, absolutely nothing, to say. I could only mutter hoarsely, "I do not think you either weak or silly, Madame."

This answer, feeble as it appeared to myself, seemed in a sense to relieve her.

She put down her paddle, leaned forward upon the front bar, with her face in her hands, and sobbed gently for a few minutes. Then, while I gazed upon her in rapt commiseration, she all at once resumed the paddle briskly.

For my own part, being just lately returned from a long expedition, my muscles were like steel; I felt that I should never weary. Steadily onward we pressed, past the mouths of several small streams whose names I did not know, past headland after headland of red clay or pallid plaster rock. As the tide fell, we were driven far out into the bay, till sometimes there was a mile of oozy red flats parting us from the edge of the green. But as the tide rose again, we accompanied its seething vanguard, till at last we were again close in shore. A breeze soon after midday springing up behind us, we made excellent progress. But soon after sunset a mist arose, which made our journey too perilous to be continued. I turned into a narrow cove between high banks, where the brawling of a shallow brook promised us fresh water. And there, in a thicket of young fir trees growing at the foot of a steep bank, I set up the canoe on edge, laid some poles and branches against it, and had a secluded shelter for my lady. She looked at it with a gratified admiration and could never be done with thanking me.

Being now near the Shubenacadie mouth, I durst not light a fire, but we uncomplainingly ate our black bread; and then I said:

"We will start at first gray, comrade. You will need all the sleep you can win. Good night, and kindly dreams."

"Good night, Monsieur," she said softly, and disappeared. Then going down to the water's side, I threw off my clothes, and took a swift plunge which steadied and refreshed me mightily. Swimming in the misty and murmurous darkness, my venture and my strange fellowship seemed more like a dream to me than ever, and I could scarce believe myself awake. But I was awake enough to feel it when, in stumbling ashore, I scraped my foot painfully on a jagged shell.   However, that hurt was soon eased and staunched by holding it for a little under the chill gushing of the brook; after which I dressed myself, gathered a handful of ferns for a pillow, and laid myself down across the opening which led into the thicket.

My Comrade Shoots Excellently Well

FROM a medley of dreams, in which I saw Mizpah binding the Black Abbé with cords of her own hair — tight, tighter, till they ate into his flesh, and I trembled at the look of shaking horror in his face; in which then I saw the child chasing butterflies before the door of the Forge in the Forest, and heard Babin's hammer beating musically on his anvil, till the sound became the chiming of the Angelus over the roofs and walls of Quebec, where Mizpah and I walked hand fast together on the topmost bastion, — from such a fleeting and blending confusion as this, I woke to feel a hand laid softly on my face in the dark. I needed no seeing to tell me whose was the hand, so slim, so cool, so softly firm;

and I had much ado to keep my lips from reverently kissing it.

"Monsieur, Monsieur," came the whisper, "what is that noise, that voice?"

"Pardon me, comrade, for sleeping so soundly," I murmured, sitting up, and taking her hand in mine with a rough freedom of goodwill, as merely to reassure her. "What is it you hear?"

But before she could reply, I heard it myself, a strange, chanting cry, slow and plangent, from far out upon the water. Presently I caught the words, and knew the voice.

"Woe, woe to Acadie the fair," it came solemnly, "for the day of her desolation draws nigh!"

"It is Grûl," said I, "passing in his canoe, on some strange errand of his."

"Grûl? Who is Grûl?" she questioned, clinging a little to my hand, and then dropping it suddenly.

"A quaint madman of these parts," said I; "and yet I think his madness is in some degree a feigning. He has twice done me inestimable service — once warning us of an immediate peril, and again yesterday, in leading us to the spot where you were held captive. For some reason unknown to me, he has a marvellous kindness for me and mine. But the Black Abbé he hates in deadly fashion — for some ancient and ineffaceable wrong, if the tale tell true."

"And he brought you to us?" she murmured, with a sort of stillness in her voice, which caught me strangely.

"Yes, Grûl did!" said I.

And then there was silence between us, and we heard the mysterious and solemn voice passing, and dying away in the distance. My ears at last being released from the tension of listening, my eyes began to serve me, and through the branches I marked a grayness spreading in the sky.

"We must be stirring, Madame," said I, rising abruptly to my feet. "Let us take our bread down to the brook and eat it there."

But she was already gone, snatching up the sack of bread; and in a few minutes, having righted the canoe and carried it down to a convenient landing-place, I joined her. She was stretched flat beside a little basin of the brook, her cap off, her hair in a tight coil high upon her head, her sleeves pulled up, while she splashed her face and arms in the running coolness. Without pulling down her sleeves or resuming her cap, she seated herself on a stone and held out to me a piece of bread. In the coldly growing dawn her hair and lips were colourless, the whiteness of her arms shadowy and spectral. Then as we slowly made our meal, I bringing water for her in my drinking-horn, the rose and fire and violet of sunrise began to sift down into our valley and show me again the hues of life in Mizpah's face. I sprang up, handed her the woollen cap, and tried hard to keep my eyes from dwelling upon the sweet and gracious curves of her arms.

"Aboard! Aboard!" I cried, and moved off in a bustling fashion to get the paddles. In a few minutes we were under way, thrusting out from the shore, and pushing through myriad little curling wisps of vapour, which rose in pale hues of violet and pink all over the oil-smooth surface of the tide.

For some time we paddled in silence. Then, when the sun's first rays fell fairly upon us, I exclaimed lightly :—

"You must pull down your sleeves, comrade."

"Why?" she asked quickly, turning her head and pausing in her stroke.

"For two excellent reasons besides the captain's orders," said I. "In the first place, your arms will get so sore with sunburn, that you won't be able to do your fair share of the work. In the second place, if we should meet any strangers, it would be difficult to persuade them that those arms were manly enough for a wood-ranger."

"Oh," she said quickly, and pulled down the sleeves in some confusion.

All that morning we made excellent progress, with the help of a light following wind. When the sun was perhaps two hours high, the mouth of the Shubenacadie opened before us; and because this river was the great highway of the Black Abbé's red people, I ran the canoe in shore and concealed it till I had climbed a bluff near by and scanned the lower reaches of the stream. Finding all clear, we put out again, and with the utmost haste paddled past the mouth. Not till we were behind the further point, and running along under the shelter of a high bank, did I breathe freely. Then I praised Mizpah, for in that burst of speed her skill and force had amazed me.

But she turned upon me with the question which I had looked for.

" If that is the Black Abbé's river," said she, with great eyes fixing mine, " and the Indians have gone that way, why do we pass by ? "

" I owe you an explanation, comrade," said I. " I think in all likelihood, that way leads straight to your child; but if we went that way, we would be the Abbé's prisoners within the next hour,—and how would we help the child then? Oh, no; I am bound for the Black Abbé's back door. A few leagues beyond this lies the River des Saumons, and on its banks is a settlement of our Acadian folk. Many of them are of the Abbé's following, and all fear him; but I have there two faithful men who are in the counsels of the Forge. One of these dwells some two miles back from the river, half a league this side of the village. I will go to him secretly, and send him on to the Shubenacadie for information. Then we will act not blindly."

To this of course she acquiesced at once, as being the only wise way; but for all that, with each canoe-length that we left the Shubenacadie behind, the more did her paddle lag. The impulse seemed all gone out of her. Soon therefore I bade her lay down the blade and rest. In a little, when she had lain a while with her face upon her arms,—whether waking or not I could not tell, for she kept her face turned away from me,—she became herself again.

No long while after noon, we ran into the mouth of the des Saumons. I was highly elated with the success that had so far attended us,—the speed we had made, our immunity from hindrance and question. We landed to eat our hasty meal, but paused not long to rest, being urged now by the keen spur of imagined nearness to our goal. Some two hours more of brisk paddling brought us to a narrow and winding creek, up which I turned. For some furlongs it ran through a wide marsh, but at length one bank grew high and copsy. Here I put the canoe to land, and stepped ashore, bidding Mizpah keep her place.

Finding the spot to my liking, I pulled the canoe further up on the soft mud, and astonished Mizpah by telling her that I must carry her up the bank.

"But why?" she cried. "I can walk, Monsieur, as well as I could this morning—though I *am* a little stiff," she added naïvely.

"The good soldier asks not why," said I, with affected severity. "But I will tell you. In case any one *should* come in my absence, there must be but one track visible, and that track mine, leading up and away toward the settlement. You must lie hidden in that thicket, and keep guard. Do you understand, Madame?"

"Yes," said she, — "but how can you? — I am awfully heavy."

I laughed softly, picked her up as I would a child, and carried her to the edge of the woods, where I let her down on one end of a fallen tree.

"Now, comrade," said I, "if you will go circumspectly along this log you will leave no trace. Hide yourself in the thicket there close to the canoe, keep your pistols primed, and watch till I come back, — and the blessed Virgin guard you!" I added, with a sudden fervour.

Then, having lifted the canoe altogether clear of the water, I set forth at a swinging trot for Martin's farm.

I found my trusty habitant at home, and ready to do any errand of mine ere I could speak it. But when I told him what I wanted of him he started in some excitement.

"Why, Monsieur," he cried, "I have the very tidings you seek. I myself saw a canoe with two Indians pass up the river this morning; and they had a little child with them, — a child with long yellow hair."

"Up *this* river!" I exclaimed. "Then whither can they be taking him?"

"They did not leave him in the village," answered Martin, positively, "for the word goes that they passed on up in great haste. By the route they have taken, they are clearly bound for the Straits —"

"Ay, they'll cross to the head of the Pictook, and descend that stream," said I. "But which way will they turn then?" — For I was surprised and confused at the information.

"Well, Monsieur," said Martin, "when they get to the Straits, who knows? They may be going across to Ile St. Jean. They may turn south to Ile Royale; for the English, I hear, have no hold there, save at Louisburg and Canseau. Or they may turn north toward Miramichi. Who knows — save the Black Abbé?"

"I must overtake them," said I, resolutely. "Good-bye, my friend and thank you. If all goes well, you will get a summons from the Forge ere the moon is again at the full;" and I made haste back to the spot where Mizpah waited.

As I swung along, I congratulated myself on the good fortune which had so held me to the trail. Then I fell to thinking of my comrade, and the wonder of the situation, and the greater wonder of her eyes and hair, — which thoughts sped the time so sweetly that ere I could believe it I saw before me the overhanging willows, and the thicket by the stream. Then I stopped as if I had been struck in the face, and shook with a sudden fear.

At my very feet, fallen across the dead tree which I have already mentioned, lay the body of an Indian. Every line of the loose, sprawled body told me that he had met an instant death, — and a bullet hole in his back showed me the manner of it. Only for a second did I pause. Then I sprang into the thicket, with a horror catching at my heart. There was Mizpah lying on her face, — and a hoarse cry broke from my lips. But even as I flung myself down beside her I saw that she was not dead. No, she was shaking with sobs,—and· the naturalness of it, strange to say, reassured me on the instant. I made to lift her, when she sprang at once to her feet, and· looked at me wildly. I took her hand, to comfort her; but she drew it away, and gazed upon it with a kind of shrinking horror.

I understood now what had happened. Nevertheless, knowing not just the best thing to say, I asked her what was the matter.

"Oh," she cried, covering her eyes, "I killed him. He threw up his hands, and groaned, and fell like a log. How could I do it? How could I do it?"

I tried to assure her that she had done well; but finding that she would pay me no heed, I went to look at her victim. I turned him over, and muttered a thanksgiving to Heaven as I recognized him for one of the worst of the Black Abbé's flock. I found his tracks all about the canoe. Then I went back to Mizpah.

"Good soldier! Good comrade!" said I, earnestly. "You have killed Little Fox, the blackest and cruelest rogue on the whole Shubenacadie. Oh, I tell you you have done a good deed this day!"

The knowledge of this appeared to ease her somewhat, and in a few moments I gathered the details. The Indian had come suddenly to the bank, and seeing a canoe there had examined it curiously,— she, the while, waiting in great fear, for she had at once recognized him as one of her former captors, and one of whom she stood in special dread. While looking at our things in the canoe, he had appeared all at once to understand. He had picked up my coat, and examined it carefully,— and the grin that disclosed his long teeth disclosed also that he recognized it. Looking to the priming of his musket, he started cautiously up the bank upon my trail.

"As soon as he left the canoe," said

Mizpah, still shaken with sobs, "I knew that something must be done. If he went away, it would be just to give the alarm, and then we could not escape, and Philip would be lost forever. But I saw that, instead of going away, he was going to track you and shoot you down. I didn't know what to do, or how I could ever shoot a man in cold blood,— but something *made* me do it. Just as he reached the end of the log, I seemed to see him already shooting you, away in the woods over there,— and then I fired. And oh, oh, oh, I shall never forget how he groaned and fell over!" And she stared at her right hand.

"Comrade," said I, "I owe my life to you. He *would* have shot me down; for, as I think of it, I went carelessly, and seldom looked behind when I got into the woods. To be so incautious is not my way, believe me. I know not how it was, unless I so trusted the comrade whom I had left behind to guard my trail. And now, here are news! They have brought the child this way, up this very river! The saints have surely led us thus far, for we are hot upon their track!"

And this made her forget to weep for the excellence of her shooting.

Chapter XV

Grûl's Hour

THOUGH we were in a hot haste to get away, it was absolutely necessary first to bury the dead Indian, lest a hue and cry should be raised that might involve and delay us. With my paddle, therefore, I dug him a shallow grave in the soft mud at the edge of the tide, which was then on the ebb. This meagre inhumation completed, I smoothed the surface as best I could with my paddle; and then we set off, resting easy in the knowledge that the next tide would smooth down all traces of the work.

It was by this close upon sunset, and I felt a little hesitation as to what we had best do. I had no wish to run through the settlement till after dark, nor was I anxious to push on against the furious

ebb of the des Saumons, against which the
strongest paddlers could make slow head-
way.   But it was necessary to get out of
the creek before the water should quite
forsake us; and, moreover, Mizpah was
in a fever of haste to be gone.   She
kept gazing about as if she expected
the savage to rise from his muddy grave
and point at her.   We ran out of the
creek, therefore, and were instantly caught
in the great current of the river.   I suffered it to sweep us down for half a mile,
having noted on the way up a cluster of
haystacks in an angle of the dyke.   Coming to these, I pushed ashore at once, carried the canoe up, and found that the
place was one where we might rest secure.
Here we ate our black bread and drank
new milk, for there were many cattle pas-
turing on the aftermath, and some of the
cows had not yet gone home to milking.
Then, hiding the canoe behind the dyke,
and ourselves between the stacks, in great
weariness we sought our sleep.

There was no hint of dawn in the sky
when I awoke with a start; but the con-

stellations had swung so wide an arc that I knew morning was close at hand. There was a hissing clamour in the river-bed which told me the tide was coming in. That, doubtless, was the change which had so swiftly aroused me. I went to the other side of the stack, where Mizpah lay with her cheek upon her arm, her hair fallen adorably about her neck. Touching her forehead softly with my hand, I whispered : —

" Come, comrade, the tide has turned ! " Whereupon she sat up quietly, as if this were for her the most usual of awakenings, and began to arrange her hair. I went out upon the shadowy marsh and soon accomplished a second theft of new milk, driving the tranquil cow which furnished it into the corner behind the stacks, that our dairy might be the more conveniently at hand. Our fast broken (and though I hinted nought of it to Mizpah, I found black bread growing monotonous), I carried the canoe down to the edge of the tide. But Mistress Mizpah's daintiness revolted at the mud, whereupon she took off her moccasins and stockings before she came to it, and I caught a gleam of slim white feet at the dewy edge of the grass. When I had carried down the paddles, pole, and baggage, I found her standing in a quandary. She could not get into the canoe with that sticky clay clinging to her feet, and there was no place where she could sit down to wash them. Carelessly enough (though my heart the while trembled within me), I stretched out my hand to her, saying:—

"Lean on me, comrade, and then you can manage it all right."

And so it was that she managed it; and so indifferently did I cast my eyes about, now at the breaking dawn, now at the swelling tide, that I am sure she must have deemed that I saw not or cared not at all how white and slender and shapely were her feet!

In few minutes we were afloat, going swiftly on the tide. The sky was all saffron as we slipped through the settlement, and a fairy glow lay upon the white cottages. The banks on either hand took

on the ineffable hues of polished nacre.
To the door of one cottage, close by the
water, came a man yawning, and hailed
us.   But I flung back a mere "*Bon jour*,"
and sped on.   Not till the settlement was
out of sight behind us, not till the cross
on the spire of the village was quite cut
off from view, did I drop to the even pace
of our day-long journeying.   When at
length we got beyond the influence of the
tide, des Saumons was a shallow, sparkling,
singing stream, its bed aglow with ruddy-
coloured rocks.   Here I laid aside my
paddle and thrust the canoe onwards by
means of my long pole of white spruce,
while Mizpah had nought to do but lean
back and watch the shores creep by.

At the head of tide we had stopped to
drink and to breathe a little.   And there,
seeing an old man working in front of a
solitary cabin, I had deemed it safe to approach him and purchase a few eggs.
After this we kept on till an hour past
noon, when I stopped in a bend of the
river, at the foot of a perpendicular cliff of
red rock some seventy or eighty feet in

height.   Here was a thicket wherein we might hide both the canoe and ourselves if necessary.   The canoe I hid at once, that being a matter of the more time. Then we both set ourselves to gathering dry sticks, for it seemed to me we might here risk the luxury of a fire, with a dinner of roasted eggs.

We had gathered but a handful or two, when I heard a crashing in the underbrush at the top of the cliff; and in a second, catching Mizpah by the hand, I had dragged her into hiding.   Through a screen of dark and drooping hemlock boughs we gazed intently at the top of the cliff,—and I noted, without thinking worth while to remedy my oversight, that I had forgotten to release Mizpah's hand.

The crashing noise, mingled with some sharp outcries of rage and fear, continued for several minutes.   Then there was silence; and I saw at the brink a pointed cap stuck full of feathers, and the glare of a black and yellow cloak.

"Grûl!" I whispered, in astonishment;

and I felt an answering surprise in the tightened clasp of Mizpah's hand.

A moment more and Grûl peered over the brink, scrutinizing the upper and lower reaches of the river. He held a coil of rope, one end of which he had made fast to a stout birch tree which leaned well out over the edge.

" What is he going to do ? " murmured Mizpah, with wide eyes.

" We'll soon see! " said I, marvelling mightily.

The apparition vanished for some minutes, then suddenly reappeared close to the brink. He carried, as lightly as if it had been a bundle of straw, the body of a man, so bound about with many cords as to remind me of nothing so much as a fly in the death wrappings of some black and yellow spider. To add to the semblance, the victim was dressed in black, — and a closer scrutiny showed that he was a priest.

" It is the Black Abbé, none other," I murmured, in a kind of awe; while Mizpah shrank closer to my side with a sense of impending tragedies. "Grûl has come to his revenge!" I added.

In a business fashion Grûl knotted the end of his coil of rope about the prisoner's body, the feathers and flowers in his cap, meanwhile, nodding with a kind of satisfied rhythm. Then he lowered the swathed and helpless but silently writhing figure a little way from the brink, governing the rope with ease by means of a half-twist about a jutting stump. There was something indescribably terrifying in the sight of the fettered form swinging over the deep, with shudderings and twistings, and the safe edge not a yard length above him. I pitied him in spite of myself; and I put a hand over Mizpah's eyes that she might not see what was coming. But she pushed my hand away, and stared in a fascination.

For some moments Grûl gazed down in silence upon his victim.

I fancied I caught the soul-piercing flame of his mad eyes; but this was doubtless due to my imagination rather than to the excellence of my vision. Sud-

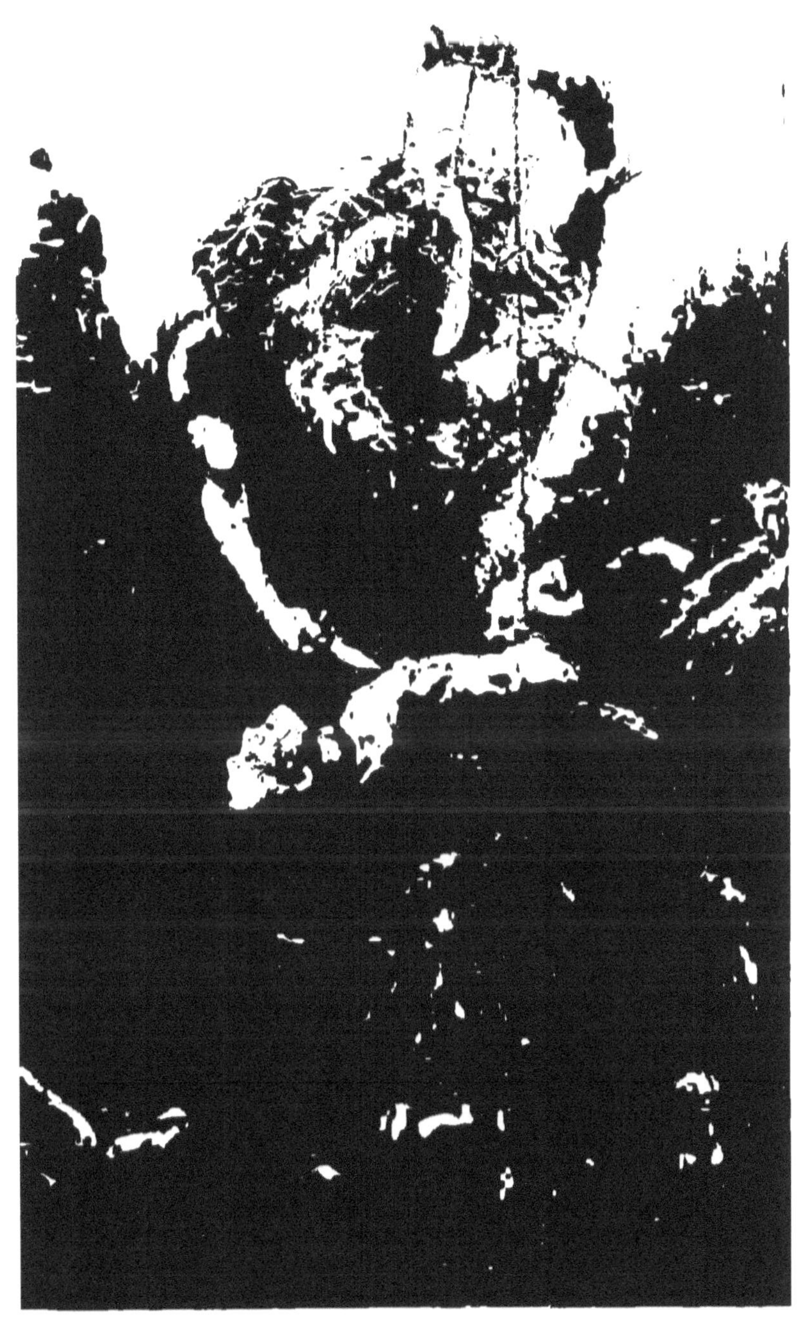

"SWINGING OVER THE DEEP, WITH SHUDDERINGS AND TWISTINGS"

denly the victim, his fortitude giving way with the sense of the deadly gulf beneath him, and with the pitiless inquisition of that gaze bent down upon him, broke out into wild pleadings, desperate entreaties, screams of anguished fear, till I myself trembled at it, and Mizpah covered her ears.

"Oh, stop it! save him!" she whispered to me, with white lips. But I shook my head. I could not reach the top of the cliff. And moreover, I had small doubt that Grûl's vengeance was just. Nevertheless, had I been at the top of the cliff instead of the bottom, I had certainly put a stop to it.

After listening for some moments, with a sort of pleasant attention, to the victim's ravings, Grûl lay flat, thrust his head and shoulders far out over the brink, and reached down a long arm. I saw the gleam of a knife in his darting hand; and I drew a quick breath of relief.

"That ends it," said I; and I shifted my position, which I had not done, as it seemed to me, for an eternity. The victim's screaming had ceased before the knife touched him.

But I was vastly mistaken in thinking it the end.

"He has not killed him," muttered Mizpah.

And then I saw that Grûl had merely cut the cord which bound his captive's hands. The Abbé was swiftly freeing himself; and Grûl, meanwhile, was lowering him down the face of the cliff. When the unhappy captive had descended perhaps twenty feet, his tormentor secured the rope, and again lay down with his head and shoulders leaning over the brink, his hands playing carelessly with the knife.

The Abbé, with many awkward gestures, presently got his limbs free, and the cord which had enwound him fell trailing like a snake to the cliff foot. Then, with clawing hands and sprawling feet, he clutched at the smooth, inexorable rock, in the vain hope of getting a foothold. It was pitiful to see his mad struggles, and the quiet of the face above looking down upon them with unimpassioned interest; till at last, exhausted, the poor wretch ceased to struggle, and looked up at his persecutor with the silence of despair.

Presently Grûl spoke, — for the first time, as far as we knew.

"You know me, Monsieur l'Abbé, I suppose," he remarked, in tone of placid courtesy.

"I know you, François de Grûl," came the reply, gasped from a dry mouth.

"Then further explanation, I think you will allow, is not needed. I will bid you farewell, and a pleasant journey," went on the same civil modulations of Grûl's voice. At the same moment he reached down with his shining blade as if to sever the rope.

"I did not do it! I did not do it!" screamed the Abbé, once more clutching convulsively at the smooth rock. "I swear to you by all the saints!"

Grûl examined the edge of his knife. He tested it with his thumb. I saw him glance along it critically. Then he touched it, ever so lightly, to the rope, so that a single strand parted.

"Swear to me," he said, in the mildest voice, "swear to me, Monsieur l'Abbé, that you had no part in it. Swear by the Holy Ghost, Monsieur l'Abbé!"

But the Abbé was silent.

"Swear me that oath now, good Abbé," repeated the voice, with a kind of courteous insistence.

"I will not swear!" came the ghastly whisper in reply.

At this an astonishing change passed over the face that peered down from the brink. Its sane tranquillity became a very paroxysm of rage. The grotesque cap was dashed aside, and Grûl sprang to his feet, waving his arms, stamping and leaping, his gaudy cloak a-flutter, his long white hair and beard twisting as if with a sentient fury of their own. He was so close upon the brink that I held my breath, expecting him to be plunged headlong. But all at once the paroxysm died out as suddenly as it had begun; and throwing himself down in his former position, Grûl once more touched the knife edge to the rope, severing fibre by fibre, slowly, slowly.

With the first touch upon the rope rose the Abbé's voice again, but no longer in vain entreaty and coward wailings. I listened with a great awe, and a sob broke from Mizpah's lips. It was the prayer for the passing soul. We heard it poured forth in steady tones but swift, against the blank face of the cliff. And we waited to see the rope divided at a stroke.

But to our astonishment, Grûl sprang to his feet again, in another fury, and flung aside his knife. With twitching hands he loosened the rope and began lowering his victim rapidly, till, within some twenty feet of the bottom, the Abbé found a footing, and stopped. Then Grûl tossed the whole rope down upon him.

"Go!" he cried in his chanting, bell-like tones. "The cup of your iniquity is not yet full. You shall not die till your soul is so black in every part that you will go down straight into hell!" And turning abruptly, he vanished.

The Black Abbé, as if seized with a faintness, leaned against the rock for some

minutes.   Then, freeing himself from the
rope, he climbed down to the foot of the
cliff, and moved off slowly by the water's
edge toward Cobequid. We trembled lest
he should see us, or the canoe, — I having
no stomach for an attack upon one who
had just gone through so dreadful a tor-
ment.   But his face, neck, ears, were like
a sweating candle ; and his contracted eyes
seemed scarce to see the ground before his
feet.

"Seemed," I say.   Yet even in this
supreme moment, he tricked me.

Chapter XVI

I Cool My Adversaries' Courage

WE now, having been so long delayed, gave up our purpose of a fire, and contented ourselves with the eggs raw. I also cut some very thin slices of the smoked and salted bacon, to eat with our black bread, for I knew that, working as we did, we needed strong food. But Mizpah would not touch the uncooked bacon, though its savour, I assured her, was excellent. We had but well begun our meal, and I was stooping over the hard loaf, when a startled exclamation from Mizpah made me look up. Close behind us stood Grûl, impatiently twisting his little white rod with the scarlet head. His eyes were somewhat more piercing, more like blue flame, than ordinarily, but otherwise he looked as usual.

So little mark remained upon him of the scene just enacted. Both wise and mad! I thought.

It struck me that he was pleased with the impression he so plainly made on us both, and for a moment he looked upon us in silence. Then swiftly pointing his stick at us, he said sharply :—

"Fools! Do you wait here? But the hound is on the trail. Do you dream he did not see you?"

Then he turned to go. But Mizpah was at his side instantly, catching him by the wrist, and imploring him to tell us which way her child had been carried.

Grûl stopped and looked down upon her with austere dignity, but without replying. Passionately Mizpah entreated him, not to be denied; and at last, lightly but swiftly removing her fingers from his wrist, he muttered oracularly :—

"They will take him to the sea that is within the heart of the land! But go!" he repeated with energy, "or you will not go far!" and with steps so smooth that they seemed not to touch the ground, he went past the cliff foot. His gaudy mantle shone for a moment, and he was gone.

The ominous urgency of his warning rang in our ears, and we were not slow in making our own departure.

"What does he mean by 'the sea that is within the heart of the land'?" asked Mizpah, as we hurriedly launched the canoe.

"He means the Bras d'Or lakes," I said, "those wonderful reaches of land-locked sea that traverse the heart of Ile Royale. It is a likely enough way for the savages to go. There are villages both of Acadians and of Indians on the island."

As we were to learn afterwards, however, Grûl had told us falsely. The child was not destined for Ile Royale. Whether the strange being really thought he was directing us aright, or, his vanity not per-mitting him to confess that he did not know, trusted to a guess with the hope that it might prove a prophecy, I have never been able to determine. As a matter of fact, Fate did presently so take our affairs into her own hands, that Grûl's misinformation affected the end not at all. But his warning and his exhortation to speed we had to thank for our escape from the perils that soon came upon us. Had we not been thus warned, without doubt we should have been taken unawares and perished miserably.

On the incidents of our journey for the rest of that day, and up to something past noon of the day following, I need not particularly dwell. Suffice to say that we accomplished prodigious things, and that Mizpah showed incredible endurance. It was as if she saw her child ever a little way before her, and hoped to come up with him the next minute. When the stream became hopelessly shallow, we got out and waded, dragging the canoe. The long portage to the head of the Pictook waters we made in the night, the trail being a clear one, and not overly rough. At the further end of the carry, when I set down the canoe at the stream's edge, I could have dropped for weariness, yet from Mizpah I heard no complaint;

and her silent heroism stirred my soul to a deepening passion of worship. Over and over I told myself that night that I would never rest or count the cost till I had given the child back to her arms.

Not till we had gone perhaps a mile down the Pictook did I order a halt, thrusting the canoe into a secure hiding-place. We snatched an hour of sleep, lying where we stepped ashore. Then, rising in the redness of daybreak, we hurried on, eating as we journeyed. And now, conceiving that it was necessary to keep up her strength, Mizpah ate of the uncooked bacon; though she wore a face of great aversion as she did so.

When, after hours of unmitigated toil, we reached the head of tide and the spacious open reaches of the lower river, I insisted on an hour of rest. Mizpah vowed that she was not exhausted, — but she slept instantly, falling by the side of the canoe as she stepped out. For myself I durst not sleep, but I rested, and watched, and sucked an egg, and chewed strips of bacon. When we pushed off again I felt that we must have put a good space between us and our pursuers; and as the ebb tide was helping me I made Mizpah go on sleeping, in her place in the bow.

"I will need your help more by and by," said I when she protested, "and then you must have all your strength to give me!"

The river soon became a wide estuary, with arms and indentations,—a harbour fit to hold a hundred fleets. Straight down mid-channel I steered, the shortest course to the mouth. But by and by there sprang up a light head-wind, delaying me.

"Wake up, comrade," I cried. "I need your good arm now, against this breeze!"

She had slept there an hour, and she woke now with a childlike flush in her cheeks.

"How good of you to let me sleep so," she exclaimed, turning to give me a grateful glance. But the expression upon her face changed instantly to one of fear, and the colour all went out.

"Oh, look behind us!" she gasped. I had not indeed waited for her words. Glancing over my shoulder, I caught sight of a large canoe, with four savages paddling furiously. The one glimpse was enough.

"Now, comrade, work!" said I. "But steady! not too hard! This is a long chase, remember!" and I bent mightily to the paddle.

Our pursuers were a good half-mile behind; and had we not been already wearied, I believe we could have held our own with them all day. Our canoe was light and swift, Mizpah paddled rarely, and for myself, I have never yet been beaten, by red man or white, in a fair canoe-race. But as it was, I felt that we must win by stratagem, if the saints should so favour us as to let us win at all. Half a mile ahead, on our right, was a high point. Behind it, as I knew, was a winding estuary of several branches, each the debouchement of a small stream. It was an excellent place in which to evade pursuers. I steered for the high point.

As we darted behind its shelter, a backward glance told me that our enemies had not gained upon us. The moment we were hidden from their view I put across to the other side of the channel, ran the canoe behind a jutting boulder, and leapt out. Not till we were concealed, canoe and all, behind a safe screen of rocks and underbrush, did Mizpah ask my purpose, though she plainly marvelled that I should hide so close to the entrance.

"A poor and something public hiding-place is often the most secret," said I. "The Indians know that up this water there are a score of turns, and backwaters, and brook-mouths, wherein we might long evade them. As soon as they saw us turn in here, they doubtless concluded that the water was well known to me, and that I would hope to baffle them in the inner labyrinths and escape up one of the streams. They will never dream of us stopping here."

"I see!" she exclaimed eagerly. "When they have passed in to look for us, we will slip out, and push on." It was haste she thought of rather than escape.   No moment passed, I think, when her whole will, her whole being, were not focussed upon the finding of the child.   And the more I realized the intensity of her love and her pain, the more I marvelled at the heroic self-control which forbade her to waste her strength in tears and wailings.   The conclusion at which she had now arrived, as to my plan, was one I had not thought of, and I considered it before replying.

"No," said I, presently; "that is not quite my purpose, though I confess it is a good one.   But, comrade, this is a safe ambush!   They must pass within close gunshot of us!"

"Oh," she cried, paling, and clasping her hands, "*must* there be more blood? But yes, they bring it on themselves," she went on with a sudden fierceness, flushing again, and her mouth growing cruel.   "They would keep us from find-ing him.   Their blood be on their own heads!"

"I am glad you think of that," said I.

"They would have no mercy for us if they should take us now. But indeed, if it will please you to have it so, we need not shoot them down. We can treat them to such a medicine as they had before of me, sink their canoe, and leave them like drowned rats on the other shore."

"Yes," said Mizpah, quietly; "if that will do as well, it will please me much better."

And so it was agreed. A very few minutes later the canoe appeared, rounding into the estuary. The savages scanned both shores minutely, but rather from the habit of caution than from any thought that we might have gone to land. If, however, I had not taken care to make my landing behind a boulder, those keen eyes would have marked some splashed spots on the shingle, and we would have been discovered.

But no such evil fortune came about. The four paddles flashed onward swiftly. The four fierce, painted and feathered heads thrust forward angrily, expecting to

overtake us in one of the inner reaches.
I took up Mizpah's musket (which was
loaded with slugs, while my own carried
a bullet, in case I should be called upon
for a long and delicate shot), and waited
until the canoe was just a little more
than abreast of us.   Then, aiming at
the waterline, just in front of the bow
paddle, I fired.

The effect was instant and complete.
The savage in the bow threw up his
paddle with a scream and sprang overboard.   He was doubtless wounded, and
feared a second shot.   We saw him swimming lustily toward the opposite shore.
The others paddled desperately in the
same direction, but before they had gone
half-way the canoe was so deep in the
water that she moved like a log.   Then
they, too, seized with the fear of a second
shot, sprang overboard.   By this time I
had the musket reloaded.

"If they get the canoe ashore, with
their weapons aboard her," said I, "they
will soon get her patched up, and we will
have it all to do over again.   Here goes

for another try, whatever heads may be in the way!"

Mizpah averted her face, but made no protest, and I fired at the stern of the canoe, which was directly toward me. A swimmer's head, close by, went down; and in a minute more the canoe did likewise. Three feathered heads remained in sight; and presently three dark figures dragged themselves ashore — one of them limping badly — and plunged into the woods.

"Without canoe or guns," said I, "they are fairly harmless for a while." But Mizpah, as we re-embarked and headed again for the sea, said nothing. I think that in her bosom, at this time, womanly compassion was striving, and at some disadvantage, with the vindictiveness of outraged motherhood. I think — and I loved her the better for it — she was glad I had killed one more of her child's enemies; but I think, too, she was filled with shame at her gladness.

Chapter XVII

A Night in the Deep

ONCE fairly out again into the harbour, I saw two things that were but little to my satisfaction. Far away up the river were three more canoes. I understood at once that the savages whom we had just worsted were the mere vanguard of the Black Abbé's attack. The new-comers, however, were so far behind that I had excellent hopes of eluding them. The second matter that gave me concern was the strong head-wind that had suddenly arisen. The look of the sky seemed to promise, moreover, that what was now a mere blow might soon become a gale. It was already kicking up a sea that hindered us. Most women would have been terrified at it, but Mizpah seemed to have no thought of fear.

We pressed on doggedly. There was danger ahead, I knew,—a very serious danger, which would tax all my skill to overcome. But the danger behind us was the more menacing. I felt that there was nothing for it but to face the storm and force a passage around the cape. This accomplished,—if we could accomplish it,—I knew our pursuers would not dare to follow.

About sundown, though the enemy had drawn perceptibly nearer, I concluded that we must rest and gather our strength. I therefore ran in behind a little headland, the last shelter we could hope for until we should get around the cape. There we ate a hearty meal, drank from a tiny spring, and lay stretched flat on the shore for a quarter of an hour. Then, after an apprehensive look at the angry sea, and a prayer that was earnest enough to make up for some scantness in length, I cried :—

"Come now, comrade, and be brave."

"I am not afraid, Monsieur," she answered quietly. "If anything happens, I know it will not be because you have failed in anything that the bravest and truest of men could hope to do."

"I think that God will help us," said I. That some one greater than ourselves does sometimes help us in such perils, I know, whatever certain hasty men who speak out of a plentiful lack of experience may declare to the contrary. But whether this help be a direct intervention of God himself, or the succour of the blessed saints, or the watchful care of one's guardian spirit, I have never been able to conclude to my own satisfaction. And very much thought have I given to the matter by times, lying out much under the stars night after night, and carrying day by day my life in my hands. However it might be, I felt sustained and comforted as we put out that night. The storm was now so wild that it would have been perilous to face in broad daylight and with a strong man at the bow paddle. Yet I believed that we should win through. I felt that my strength, my skill, my sureness of judgment, were of a sudden made greater than I could commonly account them.

But whatever strength may have been graciously vouchsafed to me that night, I found that I needed it all. The night fell not darkly, but with a clear sky, and the light of stars, and a diffused glimmer from the white crests of the waves. The gale blew right on shore, and the huge roar of the surf thundering in our ears seemed presently to blunt our sense of peril. The great waves now hung above us, white-crested and hissing, till one would have said we were in the very pit of doom. A moment more, and the light craft would seem to soar upward as the wave slipped under it, a wrenching turn of my wrist would drive her on a slant through the curling top of foam, and then we would slide swiftly into the pit again, down a steep slope of purplish blackness all alive with fleeting eyes of white light. The strain upon my wrist, the mighty effort required at each wave lest we should broach to and be rolled over, were something that I had never dreamed to endure.

Yet I did endure it. And as for the brave woman in the bow, she simply paddled on, steadily, strongly, without violence, so that I learned to depend on her for just so much force at each swift following crisis. For there was a new crisis every moment, — with a moment's grace as we slipped into each succeeding pit. At last we found ourselves off the cape, — and then well out into the open Strait, yet not engulfed. A little, — just as much as I durst, and that was very little, — I shifted our course toward south. This brought a yet heavier strain upon my wrist, but there was no help for it if we would hope to get beyond the cape. How long we were I know not. I lost the sense of time. I had no faculty left save those that were in service now to battle back destruction. But at last I came to realize that we were well clear of the cape, that the sound of the breakers had dwindled, and that the time had come to turn. To turn? Ay, but could it be done?

It could but be tried. To go on thus much longer was, I knew, impossible.

My strength would certainly fail by and by.

"Comrade," said I, — and my voice sounded strange, as if long unused, — "keep paddling steadily as you are, but the moment I say 'change,' paddle *hard* on the other side."

"Yes, Monsieur!" she answered as quietly as if we had been walking in a garden.

I watched the approach of one of those great waves which would, as I knew, have as vast a fellow to follow upon it. As soon as we were well over the crest I began to turn.

"Change!" I shouted. And Mizpah's paddle flashed to the other side. Down we slanted into the pit. We lay at the bottom for a second, broadside on, — then we got the little craft fairly about as she rose. A second more, and the wind caught us, and completed the turn, — and the next crest was fairly at my back. I drew a huge breath, praising God and St. Joseph; and we ran in toward the hollow of the land before us. That part of the coast was strange to me, save as seen when passing by ship; but I trusted there would be some estuary or some winding, within which we might safely come to land.

The strain was now different, and therefore my nerves and muscles felt a temporary relief; but it was still tremendous. There was still the imminent danger of broaching to as each wave-crest seized and twisted the frail craft. But having the wind behind me, I had of course more steerage way; and therefore a more instant and effective control. We ran on straight before the wind, but a few points off; and with desperate anxiety I peered ahead for some hint of shelter on that wild lee shore. Mizpah, of course, knew the unspeakable strain of wielding the stern paddle in such a sea.

" Are you made of steel, Monsieur ? " she presently asked. " I can hardly believe it possible that the strength of human sinews should endure so long."

" Mine, alas, will not endure much longer, comrade," said I.

"And what then?" she asked, in a steady voice.

"I do not know," said I; "but there is hope. I think we have not been brought through all this for nothing."

The roar of the breakers grew louder and louder again, as we gradually neared the high coast which seemed to slip swiftly past on our right hand. It was black and appalling, serried along the crest with tops of fir trees, white along the base with the great gnashing of the breakers. As we ran into the head of the bay, with yet no sign of a shelter, the seas got more perilous, being crowded together and broken so that I could not calculate upon them. Soon they became a mad smother; and I knew my strength for this bout had but little longer to last.

"The end!" said I; "but we may win through! I will catch you when the crash comes." And some blind prayer, I know not what, kept repeating and repeating in the inward silence of my soul. New strength seemed then to flow upon nerve and sinew, — and I descried, almost ahead of us, a space of smooth and sloping beach up which the seas rushed without rock to shatter them.

"This is our chance," I shouted. A wave came, smoother and more whole than most, and paddling desperately I kept awhile upon the crest of it. Then like a flash it curled thinly, rolled the canoe over, and hurled us far up on the beach. Half blinded, half stunned, and altogether choking, I yet kept my wits; and catching Mizpah by the arm, I dragged her violently forward beyond reach of the next wave. Dropping her without a word, I turned back, and was just in time to catch the rolling canoe. It, too, I succeeded in dragging to a place of safety; but it was so shattered and crushed as to be useless. The muskets, however, were in it; for I had taken care to lash them under the bars before leaving the shelter of the inlet.

The remnants of the canoe I hauled far up on the beach, and then I returned to Mizpah, who lay in utter exhaustion just where I had dropped her, so close to the water's edge that she was splashed by the spray of every wave.

"Come, comrade," I said, lifting her gently. "The saints have indeed been kind to us." But she made no reply. Leaning heavily upon me, and moving as if in a dream, she let me lead her to the edge of the wood, where the herbage began behind a sort of windrow of rocks. There, seeing that the rocks shut off the wind, I released her, and dropping on the spot, she went at once to sleep. Then I felt myself suddenly as weak as a baby. I had no more care for anything save to sleep. I tried to pluck a bunch of herbage to put under Mizpah's head for a pillow; but even as I stooped to gather it, I forgot where I was, and the tide of dreams flowed over me.

Chapter XVIII

The Osprey, of Plymouth

IT must have been a good two hours that I slept. I woke with a start, with a sense of some duty left undone. I was in an awkward position, half on my side amid stones and underbrush, my arms clasping the bundle of herbage which I had meant for Mizpah's pillow. The daylight was fairly established, blue and cold, though the sun was not yet visible. The gale hummed shrilly as ever, the huge waves thundered on the trembling beach, and all seaward was such a white and purple hell of raving waters that I shuddered at the sight of it. Mizpah was still sleeping. As I looked at her the desire for sleep came over me again with deadly strength, but I resisted it, rushing down to the edge of the surf, and facing a

chill buffet of driven spume. I took another glance at the canoe. It was past
mending. The two muskets were there,
but everything else was gone, washed away,
or ground upon the rocks. After much
searching, however, to my delight I found
a battered roll of bacon wedged into a
cleft. Pouncing upon this, I bore it in
triumph to Mizpah.

"Wake up, comrade," I cried, shaking her softly. "We must be getting
away."

The poor girl roused herself with diffi-
culty, and sat up. When she tried to
stand, she toppled over, and would have
fallen if I had not caught her by the
arms. It was some minutes before she
could control the stiffness of her limbs.
At last the whipping of the wind somewhat revived her, and sitting down upon
a rock she looked about with a face of
hopeless misery.

"Eat a little," said I, gently, "for we
must get away from here at once, lest
our enemies come over the hills to look
for us."

But she pushed aside the untempting, sodden food which I held out to her.

"Whither shall we go?" she asked heavily. "The canoe is wrecked. How can we find my boy? Oh, I wish I could die!"

Poor girl! my heart ached for her. I knew how her utter and terrible exhaustion had at last sapped that marvellous courage of hers; but I felt that roughness would be her best tonic, though it was far indeed from my heart to speak to her roughly.

"Shame!" said I, in a voice of stern rebuke. "Have you struggled and endured so long, to give up now? Will you leave Philip to the savages because a canoe is broken? Where is your boasted courage? Why, we will walk, instead of paddling. Come at once."

Even this rebuke but half aroused her. "I'm so thirsty," she said, looking around with heavy eyes. By good Providence, there was a slender stream trickling in at this point, and I led her to it. While she drank and bathed her face, I grubbed in the long grasses growing beside the stream, and found a handful of those tuberous roots which the Indians call ground-nuts. These I made her eat, after which she was able to endure a little of the salt bacon. Presently, she became more like herself, and began to grieve at the weakness which she had just shown. Her humiliation was so deep that I had much ado to comfort her, telling her again and again that she was not responsible for what she had said when she was yet but half awake, and in the bonds of a weariness which would have killed most women. I told her, which was nothing less than true, that I held her for the bravest of women, and that no man could have supported me better than she had done.

We pushed our way straight over the height of land which runs seaward and ends in Cape Merigomish. Our way lay through a steep but pleasant woodland, and by the time the sun was an hour high we had walked off much of our fatigue. The tree tops rocked and creaked high above us, but where we walked the wind troubled us not.

"Where are we going?" asked Mizpah, by and by — somewhat tremulously for she still had in mind my censure.

"Why, comrade," said I, in a cheerful, careless manner of speech, a thousand miles away from the devotion in my heart, — "my purpose is to push straight along the coast to Canseau. There we will find a few of your country-folk, fishermen mostly, and from them we will get a boat to carry us up the Bras d'Or."

"But what will become of Philip, all this time?" she questioned, with haggard eyes.

"As a matter of fact," I answered, "I don't think we will lose much time, after all. If we still had the canoe, we would be storm-bound in the bay back there till the wind changes or subsides — and it may be days before it does the one or the other. As it is, the worst that has befallen us is the loss of our ammunition and our bread. But we will make shift to live, belike, till we reach Canseau."

"Oh, Monsieur," she cried, in answer, with a great emotion in her voice, "you give me hope when my despair is blackest. You seem to me more generous, more brave, more strong, than I had dreamed the greatest could be. What makes you so good to an unhappy mother, so faithfully devoted to a poor baby whom you have never seen?"

"Tut, tut!" said I, roughly; "I but do as any proper minded man would do that had the right skill and the fitting opportunity. Thank Marc!" But I might have told her more if I had let my heart speak truth.

"I know whom to thank, and all my life long will I pray Heaven to bless that one!" said Mizpah.

Thus talking by the way, but most of the way silent, we came at length over Merigomish and down to the sea again, fetching the shore at the head of a second bay. This was all in a smother and a roar, like that we had just left behind. As we rounded the head of it, we came upon a little sheltered creek, and there,

safe out of the gale, lay a small New England fishing schooner. I knew her by the
build for a New Englander, before I saw
the words OSPREY, PLYMOUTH, painted in
red letters on her stern.

"Here is fortune indeed!" said I,
while a cry of gladness sprang to Mizpah's lips. "I'll charter the craft to take
us up the Bras d'Or."

The little ship lay in a very pleasant
idleness. The small haven was full of
sun, the green, wooded hills sloping softly
down about it and shutting off all winds.
The water heaved and rocked; but
smoothly, stirred by the yeasty tumult
that roared past the narrow entrance.
The clamour of the surf outside made the
calm within the more excellent.

Several gray figures of the crew lay
sprawling about the deck, which we could
see very well, by reason of the steepness
of the shore on which we stood. In the
waist was a gaunt, brown-faced man, with
a scant, reddish beard, a nose astonishingly
long and sharp, and a blue woollen cap on
the back of his head. He stood leaning

upon the rail watching us, and spitting contemplatively into the water from time to time.

We climbed down to the beach beside the schooner, and I spoke to the man in English.

"Are you the captain?" I asked civilly.

"They do say I be," he answered in a thin, high, sing-song of a voice. "Captain Ezra Bean, Schooner *Osprey*, of Plymouth, at your sarvice." And he waved his hand with a spacious air.

I bowed with ceremony. "And I am your very humble servant," said I, "the Sieur de Briart, of Canard by Grand Pré. We were on our way to Canseau, but have lost our canoe and stores in the gale. We are bold to hope, Captain, that you will sell us some bread, as also some powder and bullets. We did not lose our little money, Heaven be praised!"

Knowing these New Englanders to be greedy of gain, but highly honest, I made no scruple of admitting that we had money about us.

"Come right aboard, good sirs!" said the captain; and in half a minute the gig, which floated at the stern, was thrust around to us, and we clambered to the deck of the *Osprey*, where crew and captain, five in all, gathered about us without ceremony. The captain, I could see at once, was just one of themselves, obeyed when he gave orders, but standing in no sort of formal aloofness. Cold salt beef, and biscuit and cheese, and tea, were soon set before us, and as we made a hasty meal they all hung about us and talked, as if we had been in one of their home kitchens on Massachusetts Bay. As for Mizpah, who felt little at ease in playing her man's part, she spoke only in French, and made as if she knew no word of English. Captain Ezra Bean had some French, but no facility in it, and a pronunciation that was beyond measure execrable.

But at last, being convinced that they were honest fellows, I spoke of chartering the *Osprey*, and in explanation told the main part of our story, representing Mizpah as a youth of Canard. But, alas, I had not read my men aright. Honest they were, and exceeding eager to turn an honest penny, — but they had not the stomach for fighting. When they found that a war party of Micmacs was in chase of us, they fell into a great consternation, and insisted on our instant departure.

At this I was all taken aback, for I had ever found the men of New England as diligent in war as in trade. But these fellows were in a shaking terror for their lives and for their ship.

"Why, gentlemen," I said, in a heat, "here are seven of us, well armed! We will make short work of the red rascals, if they are so foolhardy as to attack us."

But no! They would hear none of it.

"It's no quarrel of mine!" cried Captain Ezra Bean, in his high sing-song, but in a great hurry. "My dooty's to my ship. There's been many of our craft fell afoul of these here savages, and come to grief. We're fast right here till the wind changes, and we'll just speak the redskins fair if they come nigh us, an' there ain't goin' to be no trouble. But you must go your ways, gentlemen, begging your pardon; and no ill will, I hope!" And the boat being hauled around for us, they all made haste to bid us farewell.

Mizpah, with a flushed face, stepped in at once; but I hung back a little, sick with their cowardly folly.

"At least," said I, angrily, "you must sell me a sack of bread, and some powder and ball. Till I get them I swear I will not go."

"Sartinly!" sing-songed the captain; and in a twinkling the supplies were in the boat. "Now go, and God speed ye!"

I slipped a piece of gold into his hand, and was off. But frightened as he was, he was honest, and in half a minute he called me back.

"Here is your silver," came the queer, high voice over the rail. "You have overpaid me three times," and I saw his long arm reaching out to me.

"Keep it," I snapped. "We are in more haste to be gone than you to get rid of us."

In five minutes more the woods en-
folded us, and the little *Osprey* was hid
from our view. I walked violently in
my wrathful disappointment, till at last
Mizpah checked me. "If the good soldier," said she, "might advise his captain,
which would be, of course, intolerable, I
would dare to remind you of what you
have said to me more than once lately.
Is not this pace too hot to last, Monsieur?" And stopping, she leaned heavily on her musket.

"Forgive me," I exclaimed, flinging
myself down on the moss. "And what
a fool I am to be angry, too, just because
those poor bumpkins wouldn't take up
our quarrel."

The look of gratitude which Mizpah
gave me for that little phrase, "our quarrel," made my heart on a sudden strong
and light. Presently we resumed our
journey, going moderately, and keeping
enough inland to avoid the windings of
the coast. The little *Osprey* we never saw
again; but months later, when it came to
my ears that a fishing vessel of Plymouth

had been taken by the Indians that autumn while storm-stayed at Merigomish, and her crew all slain, I felt a qualm of pity for the poor lads whose selfish fears had so misguided them.

Chapter XIX

The Camp by Canseau Strait

IT was perhaps to their encounter with the *Osprey* we owed it that we saw no more of our pursuers. At any rate we were no further persecuted. After two days of marching we felt safe to light fires.

We shot partridges, and a deer; and the fresh meat put new vigour into our veins. We came to the beginning of the narrow strait which severs Ile Royale from the main peninsula of Acadie; and with longing eyes Mizpah gazed across, as if hoping to discern the child amid the trees of the opposite shore. At last, I could but say to her : —

" We are a long, long way from Philip yet, my comrade ; were we across this narrow strait, we would be no nearer to him, for the island is so cut up with inland waters, many, deep, and winding, that it would take us months to traverse its length afoot. We must push on to Canseau, for a boat is needful to us."

And all these days, in the quiet of the great woods, in the stillness of the wilderness nights when often I watched her sleeping, in the hours while she walked patiently by my side, her brave, sweet face wan with grief suppressed, her eyes heavy with longing, my love grew. It took possession of my whole being till this doubtful, perilous journey seemed all that I could desire, and the world we had left behind us became but a blur with only Marc's white face in the midst to give it consequence. Nevertheless, though my eyes and my spirit waited upon all her movements, I suffered no least suggestion of my worship to appear, but ever with rough kindliness played the part of companion-at-arms.

One morning, — it was our fifth day from the *Osprey*, but since reaching the Strait we had become involved in swamps, and made a very pitifully small advance,

—one morning, I say, when it wanted perhaps an hour of noon, we were both startled by a sound of groaning. Mizpah came closer to me, and put her hand upon my arm. We stood listening intently.

" It is some one hurt," said I, in a moment, " and he is in that gully yonder."

Cautiously, lest there should be some trap, we followed the sound ; and we discovered, at the bottom of a narrow cleft, an Indian lad lying wedged between sharp rocks, with the carcass of a fat buck fallen across his body. It was plain to me at once that the young savage had slipped while staggering under his load of venison.

I hesitated ; for what more likely than that there should be other Indians in the neighbourhood ; but Mizpah cried at once : —

"Oh, we must help him ! Quick ! Come, Monsieur ! "

And in truth the lad's face appealed to me, for he was but a stripling, little younger than Marc. Very gently we released him from his agonizing position ; and when we had laid him on a patch of smooth moss, his groaning ceased. His lips were parched, and when I brought him water he swallowed it desperately. Then Mizpah bathed his face. Presently his eyes opened, rested upon her with a look of unutterable gratitude, and closed again. Mizpah's own eyes were brimming with tears, and she turned to me in a sort of appeal, as if she would say : —

"How can we leave him?"

"Let him be for a half hour now," said I, answering her look. "Then perhaps he will be able to talk to us."

We ate our meal without daring to light a fire. Then we sat in silence by the sleeping lad, till at last he opened his eyes, and murmured in the Micmac tongue, "water." When he had taken a drink, I offered him biscuit, of which he ate a morsel. Then, speaking in French, I asked him whence he came; and how he came to be in such a plight.

He answered faintly in the same tongue. "I go from Malpic," said he, "to the Shubenacadie, with messages. I shot a buck, on the rock there, and he fell into the gully. As I was getting him out I fell in myself, and the carcass on top of me. I know no more till I open my eyes, and my mouth is hard, and kind friends are giving me water. Then I sleep again, for I feel all safe," and with a grateful smile his eyes closed wearily. He was fast asleep again, before I could ask any more questions.

"Come away," I whispered to Mizpah, "till we talk about this." She came, but first, with a tender thoughtfulness, she leaned her musket against a tree, with his own beside it, so that if he should wake while we were gone he should at once see the two weapons, and know that he was not deserted.

When we were out of earshot, I turned and looked into her eyes.

"What is to be done with him?" I asked.

"We must stay and take care of him," said she, steadily, "till he can take care of himself."

"And Philip?" I questioned.

She burst into tears, flung herself down, and buried her face in her hands. After sobbing violently for some minutes she grew calm, dashed her tears away, and looked at me in a kind of despair.

"The poor boy cannot be left to die here alone," she said, in a shaken voice. "It is perfectly plain what we must do. Oh, God, take care of my poor lonely little one." And again she covered her eyes. I took one of her hands in mine, and pressed it firmly.

"If there is justice in Heaven, he will," I cried passionately. "And he will; I know he will. I think there never was a nobler woman than you, my comrade."

"You do not know me," she answered, in a low voice; and rising, she returned to the sick boy's side.

Seeing that we were here for some days, or perchance a week, I raised two hasty shelters of brush and poles. That night the patient wandered in his mind, but in the morning the fever had left him, and thenceforward he mended swiftly. His gratitude and his docility were touching, and his eyes followed Mizpah as would the eyes of a faithful dog. I think his insight penetrated her disguise, so that from the first he knew her for a woman; but his native delicacy kept him from betraying his knowledge. As far as I could see, there were no bones broken, and I guessed that in a week at furthest he would be able to resume his journey without risk.

For three days I troubled him not with further questions, Mizpah having so decreed. She said that questioning would hinder his recovery; but I think she feared what questioning might disclose. At last, as we finished supper, of which he had well partaken, he rose feebly but with determination, took a few tottering paces, and then came back to his couch, where he lay with gleaming eyes of satisfaction.

" I walk now pretty soon," said he. "Not keep kind friends here much longer. Which way you going when you stopped to take care of Indian boy?"

I looked across at Mizpah, then made up my mind to speak plainly. If I knew anything at all of human nature, this boy was to be trusted.

"We are going to Ile Royale," said I, "to look for a little boy whom some of your tribe have cruelly carried off."

His face became the very picture of shame and grief. He looked first at one of us, then the other; and presently dropped his head upon his breast.

"Why, what is the matter, Xavier?" I asked. He had said his name was Xavier.

"I know," he answered, in a low voice. "It was some of my own people did it."

"*What* do you know? Tell us, oh, tell us everything! Oh, we helped you! You will surely help us find him!" pleaded Mizpah, breathlessly.

"By all the blessed saints," he cried, with an earnestness that I felt to be sincere, "I will try to help you. I will risk anything. I will disobey the Abbé. I will—"

"Where *is* the child? Do you know that?" I interrupted.

"Yes, truly," he replied. "They have taken him north to Gaspé, and to the St. Lawrence. My uncle, Etienne le Bâtard, was in canoe that brought him to mouth of the Pictook. Then other canoe took him north, where a French family will keep him. The Abbé says he shall grow up a monk. But he is not starved or beaten, I swear truly."

"How do you know all this?" I asked, looking at him piercingly. But his eye was clear and met mine right honestly.

"My uncle came to Malpic straight," said he, "where the warriors had a council. Then I was sent with word to my father, Big Etienne, who is on the Shubenacadie."

"What word?" I asked.

But the boy shook his head. "It does not touch the little boy. It does not touch my kind friends. I may not tell it," he said, with a brave dignity. I loved him for this, and trusted him the more.

"This lad's tongue and heart are true," said I, looking at Mizpah. "We may trust him."

"I know it!" said she. Whereupon

he reached out, grasped a hand of each, and kissed them with a freedom of emotion which I have seldom seen in the full blood Indian.

"You may trust me," he said, in a low voice, being by this something wearied. "You give me my life. And I will help you find your child."

And the manner of his speech, as if he considered the child *our* child, though it was but accident, stirred me sweetly at the heart,—and I durst not trust myself to meet Mizpah's eyes.

Thus it came about that, after all, we crossed not the narrow strait, nor set foot in Ile Royale. But when, three days later, I judged our patient sufficiently recovered, we set our faces again toward the Shubenacadie.

The journey was exceeding slow, but to me very far from tedious, for in rain or shine, or dark or bright, the light shone on me of my mistress's face.

And at last, after many days of toilsome wandering, we struck the head waters of the Shubenacadie.

From this point forward we went with more caution. When we were come within an hour of the Indian village, Xavier parted company with us. The river here making a long loop, so to speak, we were to cross behind the village at a safe distance, strike the tide again, and hide at a certain point covered with willows till Xavier should bring us a canoe.

We reached the point, hid ourselves among the willows, and waited close upon two hours. The shadows were falling long across the river, and our anxieties rising with more than proportioned speed, when, at last, a canoe shot around a bend of the river, and made swiftly for the point. We saw Xavier in the bow, but there was a tall, powerful warrior in the stern. As the canoe drew near, Mizpah caught me anxiously by the arm.

"That man was one of the band that captured us at Annapolis," she whispered. "What does it mean? *Could* Xavier mean to — ?"

"No," I interrupted; "of course not, comrade. These Indians are never treacherous to those who have earned their gratitude. Savages though they be, they set civilization a shining example in that. There is nothing to fear here."

Landing just below us, the two Indians came straight toward our hiding-place. At the edge of the wood the tall warrior, whom I now knew for a certainty to be Big Etienne himself, stopped, and held out both his hands, palm upwards. I at once stepped forth to meet him, leaving my musket behind me. But Mizpah who followed me closely, clung to hers,— which might have convinced me, had I needed conviction, that hero though she was she was yet all woman.

"You my brother and my sister!" said the tall warrior at once, speaking with dignity, but with little of Xavier's fluency. He knew Mizpah.

"I am glad my brother's heart is turned towards us at last," said I. "My brother knows what injury has been done to us, and what we suffer at the hands of his people."

"Listen," said he, solemnly. "You

give me back my son, my only son, my
young brave," and he looked at Xavier
with loving pride; " for that I can never
pay you; but I give you back your son,
too, see?   And, now, always, I am your
brother.   But now, you go home.   I find
the child away north, by the Great River.
I put him in your arms, safe, laughing,
—so;" and he made as if to place a little
one in Mizpah's arms.   " Then you believe I love you, and Xavier love you.
But now, come; not good to stay here
more."   And, turning abruptly, he led
the way to the canoe, and himself taking
the stern paddle, while Xavier took the
bow, motioned us to get in.   I hesitated;
whereupon he cried : —

" Many of our people out this way.
River not safe for you now. We take you
to Grand Pré, Canard, Pereau, — where
you want. Then go north. Better so."

Seeing the strong reason in his words, I
accepted his offer thankfully, but insisted
upon taking the bow myself, because
Xavier was not yet well enough to paddle
strongly.

Thus we set out, going swiftly with the tide. As we journeyed, Big Etienne was at great pains to make us understand that it would take him many weeks to find Philip and bring him back to us, because the way was long and difficult. He said we must not look to see the lad before the snow lay deep ; but he bound himself to bring him back in safety, barring visitation of God. I saw that Mizpah now trusted the tall warrior even as I did. I felt that he would make good his pledge at any hazard. I urged, however, that he should take me with him ; but on this point he was obstinate, saying that my presence would only make his task the more difficult, for reasons which occurred to me very readily. It cost me a struggle to give up my purpose of being myself the child's rescuer, and so winning the more credit in Mizpah's eyes. But this selfish prompting of my heart I speedily crushed (for which I thank Heaven) when I saw that Big Etienne's plan was the best that could be devised for Philip.

Some miles below the point where the

river was already widening, we passed a group of Indians with their canoes drawn up on the shore, waiting to ascend with the returning tide. Recognizing Big Etienne in the stern, they paid us no attention beyond a friendly hail. Late in the evening we camped, well beyond the river mouth. Once on the following morning, when far out upon the bosom of the bay, we passed a canoe that was bound for the Shubenacadie, and again the presence and parting hail of our protector saved us from question. Our halts for meals were brief and far apart, but light head winds baffled us much on the journey, so that it was not till toward evening of the second day out from the Shubenacadie mouth that we paddled into the Canard, and drew up at Giraud's little landing under the bank.

Chapter XX

The Fellowship Dissolved

IN Giraud's cabin during our absence things had gone tranquilly. We found Marc mending, — pale and weak indeed, but happy; Prudence no longer pale, and with a content in her eyes which told us that her time had not been all passed in grieving for our absence. Father Fafard was in charge, of course; and of the Black Abbé there had been nothing seen or heard since our departure.

Nevertheless there was great news, and a word that deeply concerned me. De Ramezay had led his little army against Annapolis. Just ten days before had he passed up the Valley; and for me he had left an urgent message, begging me to join him immediately on my return. This was a black disappointment; for just now my soul desired nothing so much as a few days of quiet converse with Mizpah, and the chance to show her a courtesy something different from the rough comradeship of our wilderness travels. But this was not to be. It was incumbent upon me to go in the morning.

That evening was a busy one; but I snatched leisure to sit by Marc's bedside and give the dear lad a hasty outline of our adventure. The tale called a flush to his face, and breathless exclamations from Prudence; but Mizpah sat in silence, save for a faint protest once or twice when I told of her heroism, and of her noble self-sacrifice on behalf of the Indian lad. She was weighed down with a sadness which she could make no pretence to hide, — doubtless feeling the more little Philip's absence and loneliness as she contemplated Marc's joy on my return. My hands and lips ached with a longing to comfort her, but I firmly forbade myself to intrude upon her sorrow. By and by, when I spoke of my positive determination to set out for Annapolis in the early morning, both Marc and Prudence strove hard to dissuade me, crying out fervently against my going; but Mizpah said nothing more than —

"Why not take *one day*, at least, to rest?"

And I was somewhat hurt at the quiet way she said it. Said I to myself within, "She might spare me a little thought, now that she knows Philip is safe, and sure to be brought back to her."

In the morning I saw Big Etienne and Xavier set forth upon their quest, — and Mizpah stood beside me to wish them a grateful "God-speed." Pale and sad as was the exquisite Madonna face, her lips were marvellously red, and wore an unwonted tenderness. Her eyes evaded mine, — which hurt me sorely, but I was comforted a little by her word as the canoe slipped silently away.

"I wish we were going with them," said she, in a wistful voice.

It was that "we" that stirred my heart.

"Would to God we were!" said I.

Half an hour later I hung over my

dear lad's pallet, pressing his hands, and bidding him adieu, and kissing his gaunt cheeks. When at last I turned away, dashing some unexpected drops from my eyes (for I had eagerly desired his comradeship in this venture, and had dreamed of him fighting at my side), I found that Prudence and the Curé had gone down to the landing to see me off, and that Mizpah stood alone just outside the door, looking pale and tired. I think I was aggrieved that she should not take the trouble to walk down as far as the landing, — and this may have lent my voice a touch of reserve.

"Good-bye, Madame," said I, holding out my hand. "May God keep you!"

In truth it lay heavily upon my soul that she should not have one thought to spare from the child, for me. Yet I was not prepared for the way she took my farewell.

"It was 'comrade' but yesterday," she murmured, flushing, and withdrawing her hand ere I could give it an instant's pressure. But growing straightway pale again, she added with the stateliness so native to her : —

" Farewell, Monsieur. May God keep you also ! My gratitude to the most gallant of gentlemen, to the bravest and truest succourer of those in need, I must ask you to believe in without words ; for truly I have no words to express it." And with that she turned away, leaving me most sore at heart for something more than gratitude.

A few minutes later, when I had made my adieux to Father Fafard, and kissed Marc's lily maid, as was my right and duty, I had a surprise which sent me on my way something more happily. As our canoe (I had Giraud with me now) slipped round a little bluff below the settlement, I caught the flutter of a gown among the trees ; and the next instant Mizpah appeared, waving her handkerchief. She had gone a good half-mile to wave me a last God-speed.

For an instant, as I bared my head, I had a vision of her hair all down about her, a glory that I can never think of without a trembling in my throat. I saw a speaking tenderness in her Madonna face, — and I seemed to hear in my heart a call which assuredly her lips did not utter; then my eyes blurred, so hard was it to keep from turning back. I leaned my head forward for a moment on my arms, as if I had been a soft boy, but feeling the canoe swerve instantly from its course, I rose at once and resumed my paddling.

Nevertheless I turned my head ever and anon toward the shore behind, till I could catch no more the flutter of her gown among the trees.

I have wondered many times since, how Mizpah's hair chanced then to be down about her in that fashion. Did some wanton branch undo it as she came hastily through the trees? Or did her own long fingers loosen it for me?

Of de Ramezay's vain march against Annapolis I need not speak with any fulness here. The September weather was propitious, wherefore the expedition was an agreeable jaunt for the troops. But my good friend the Commander found the fort too strong and too well garrisoned for the force he had brought against it; and the great fleet from France which was to have supported him came never to drop anchor in the basin of secure Port Royal. It is an ill tale for French ears to hear, for French lips to relate, that which tells of the thronged and mighty ships which sailed from France so proudly to restore the Flag of the Lilies to her ancient strongholds. Oh, my Country, what hadst thou done, that the stars in their courses should fight against thee? For, indeed, the hand of fate upon the ships was heavy from the first. Great gales scattered them. By twos and threes they met the English foe, and were destroyed; or disease broke out amongst their crews, till they were forced to flee back into port with their dying; or they struggled on through infinite toil and pain, to be hurled to wreck on our iron capes of Acadie. The few that came in safety fled back again when

they knew the fate of their fellows. And
our grim-visaged adversaries of New England, rejoicing in their great deliverance,
set themselves to singing psalms of praise
with great lustihood through their noses.

And for my own part, when I reached
de Ramezay's camp, the enterprise was
already as good as abandoned. For a
week longer, less to annoy the enemy,
than to spy out the land and commune
with the inhabitants, we lay before Annapolis.   Then de Ramezay struck camp,
and bade his grumbling companions march
back to Chignecto.

But of me he asked a service. And,
though I had hoped to go at once to
Canard, I could not, in honour, deny him.
I saw him and his little army marching
back whither my heart was fain to drag
me also ; but my face was set seaward,
whither I had no desire to go.

For the matter was, that de Ramezay
had affairs with the Abenaqui chiefs of
the Penobscot, which affairs he was now
unable to tend in person, and which he
durst hardly entrust to a subordinate, or

to one unused to dealing with our savage allies. He knew my credit among the Penobscot tribes,—and indeed, he would have been sorely put to it, had I denied him in the matter. The affair carried me from the Penobscot country on to the St. Lawrence, and then to Montreal. The story of it is not pertinent to this narrative, and moreover, which is more to the purpose, the affair was no less private in its nature than public in its import. Suffice to say of it, therefore, that with my utmost despatch it engaged me up to the closing of the year. It was not till January was well advanced that I found myself again in de Ramezay's camp at Chignecto, and looked out across the snow-glittering marshes to the dear hills of Acadie.

I found that during my absence things had happened. The English governor at Annapolis, conceiving that the Acadians were restless to throw off the English yoke, had called upon New England for reinforcements. In answer, Boston had sent five hundred of her gaunt and silent soldiery, bitter fighters, drinkers of strong rum, quaintly sanctimonious in their cups. Their leader was one Colonel Noble, a man of excellent courage, but small discretion, and with a foolish contempt for his enemies. These men, as de Ramezay told me, were now quartered in Grand Pré village, and lying carelessly. It was his purpose to attack them at once. But being himself weak from a recent sickness, he was obliged to place the conduct of the enterprise in the hands of his second in command. This, as I rejoiced to learn, was a very capable and experienced officer, Monsieur de Villiers, — the same who, some years later, was to capture the young Virginian captain, Mr. Washington, at Fort Necessity. Though our force was less than that of the New Englanders, de Ramezay and de Villiers both trusted to the advantages of a surprise and a night attack.

For my own part I liked little this plan of a night attack; for I love a fair defiance and an open field, and all my years of bush fighting have not taught me another sentiment. But I was well inclined toward any action that would take me speedily to Canard. Moreover, I knew that de Ramezay's plan was justified by the smallness of the force which he could place at de Villiers' command. I had further a shrewd suspicion that there were enough of the villagers on the English side to keep the New Englanders fairly warned of our movements. In this, as I learned afterwards, I suspected rightly, but the blind over-confidence of Colonel Noble made the warning of no effect. The preparations for our march went on briskly, and with an eager excitement. The bay being now impassable by reason of the drifting ice, the journey was to be made on snow-shoes, by the long, circuitous land route, through Beaubassin, Cobequid, Piziquid, and so to the Gaspereau mouth. Every one was in high spirits with the prospect of action after a long and inglorious delay. But for me the days passed leadenly. I was consumed with impatience, and anxiety, and passionate desire for a face that was never an hour absent from my thoughts. My first act on arriving at Chignecto had been to ask for Tamin, trusting that he might have tidings from Canard. But de Ramezay told me that he had sent the shrewd fisherman-soldier to Grand Pré for information.

In a fever I awaited his return.

At last, but three days before the time set for our departure, he arrived. From him I learned that Marc was so far recovered as to walk abroad for a short airing whenever the weather was fine. He, as well as the ladies, was lying very close in Giraud's cottage, and their presence was not known to the New Englanders at Grand Pré, at which information I was highly gratified.

"And are the ladies in good health?" I asked.

"The little Miss looks rugged, and her eyes are like stars," said Tamin; "but Madame — Ah, she is pale, and her eyes are heavy." Tamin's own eyes almost hid themselves in a network of little wrinkles as he spoke, scrutinizing my face. "She weeps for the child. She said perhaps *you*, Monsieur, would find him in your travels, and bring him back to her!"

My heart sank at the word. I could not go to Canard, — I could not face Mizpah again, till I could go to her with Philip in my arms. I had hoped that he was restored to her ere this. What had happened? Had Big Etienne deceived me? And Xavier, too? I could not think it. Yet what else could I think?

"Ah, my friend," said I, with bitterness, "she will be grievously disappointed in me. She will say I promise much, and perform little. And alas, it seems even so. I have not seen or heard of the child. But has Big Etienne come back? *Surely* he has not come back without the child?"

Tamin, it was plain, had heard the whole story from Marc, for he asked no questions, and showed no surprise.

"No," said he, "they're both away, Big Etienne and Xavier, gone nigh onto four months. Some says to Gaspé; some says to Saguenay. Who knows? They're Injuns!" And Tamin shrugged his shoulders, while his honest little eyes grew beady with distrust.

But I no more distrusted, and my heart lightened mightily. They had been checked, baffled perhaps, for weeks; but I felt that they were faithful and would succeed. I resolved that the moment this enterprise of de Villiers' was accomplished I would go to help them. But I had yet more questions for Tamin.

"And the Black Abbé?" I asked. "Where is he?"

"At Baie Verte, minding his store, or at Cobequid with his red lambs," replied Tamin, puckering his wide mouth drolly. "He is little at Chignecto since he met *you* there, Monsieur. And he has not been seen at Canard since Giraud's cabin grew so hospitable. But Grûl is much in the neighbourhood. I think the Black Abbé fears him."

Remembering the awful scene on the cliffs of the des Saumons, I felt that

Tamin's surmise was fairly founded ; and I blessed the strange being who thus kept watch over those whom I loved. But I said nothing to Tamin of what was in my mind, thinking it became me to keep Grûl's counsel.

Chapter XXI

The Fight at Grand Pré

ON the 23d day of January, 1747, we set out from Chignecto, four hundred tried bush fighters, white and red, — some three score of our men being Indians. We went on snow-shoes, for the world was buried in drifts. There was much snow that winter, with steady cold and no January thaw. On the marsh the snow lay in mighty windrows; but in the woods it was deep, deep, and smotheringly soft. The branches of fir and spruce and hemlock bent to the earth beneath the white burden of it, forming solemn aisles and noiseless fanes within. We marched in column. The leaders, who had the laborious task of tramping the unbroken snow, would keep their place for an hour, then fall to the rear, and enjoy the grateful ease of marching in the footsteps of their fellows. Sometimes, as our column wound along like a huge dark snake, some great branch, awakened by our laughter, would let slip its burden upon us in a sudden avalanche. Sometimes, in crossing a hidden watercourse, the leading files would disappear, to be dragged forth drenched and cursing and derided.

But there were as yet no enemies to beware of; so we marched merrily, and cheered our nights with unstinted blaze of camp fires.

On our fourth evening out from Chignecto, when we had halted about an hour, there came visitors to the camp. My ear was caught by the sentry's challenge. I went indifferently to see what the stir was all about.

"Monsieur, we are come!" cried a glad voice which I keenly remembered; and Xavier, his face aglow in the firelight, sprang forward to grasp my hand. Behind him, standing in moveless dignity, was Big Etienne, and at his feet a light sledge, with a bundle wrapped in furs.

My heart gave a great bound of thankful joy; and I stepped forward to seize the tall warrior's hand in both of mine.

"He is well! He sleeps!" said Big Etienne, gravely.   In dealing with men, I pride myself on knowing what to say and how to say it.   But at this moment I was filled with so many emotions that words were not at my command.   Some sort of thanks I stammered to express, — but the Indian understood and interrupted me.

"You thank me moons ago, brother," he said, in an earnest voice.   "You give me my boy.   Now I give you yours. And we will not forget.   That's all."

"We will never forget, indeed, my brother," said I, fervently, and again I clasped hands with him, thus pledging a comradeship which in many a strait since then has stood me in good stead.

During the rest of that long mid-winter march, Philip remained in the care of young Xavier, to whom, as well as to Big Etienne, he was altogether devoted; and I saw a new side of the red man's character in the tenderness of the stern chief toward the child.   For my own part I lost no time in bidding for my share in Philip's affections.   My love went out to the brave-eyed little fellow as if he had been the child of my own flesh.   And moreover I was fain to win an ally who would help me to besiege his mother's heart.

Big Etienne had spoken within the mark in saying the child was well.   His cheeks were dark with smoke and with forgetfulness of soap and water; but the red blood tinged them wholesomely.   His long yellow hair was tangled, but it had the burnished resilience of health.   His mouth, a bow of strength and sweetness, — his mother's mouth, — wore the scarlet of clean veins; and the great sea-green eyes with which he stirred my soul were unclouded by fear or sickness.   Before our march brought us to the hills of Gaspereau, Philip had admitted me to his favour, ranking me, I think, almost as he did Xavier and Big Etienne.   More than that I could not have dared to hope.

At sundown of the ninth of February, the seventeenth day of our march from

Chignecto, we halted in a fir wood only three miles from the Gaspereau mouth. We lit no camp fires now, but supped cold, though heartily. We had been met the day before by messengers from Grand Pré, who told de Villiers the disposition of the English troops. With incredible carelessness they were scattered throughout the settlement. About one hundred and fifty, under Colonel Noble himself, were quartered along a narrow lane, which, running at right angles to the main street, climbed the hillside at the extreme west of the village. For my own part, though de Villiers' senior in military rank, I was but a volunteer in this expedition, and served the chief as a kind of informal aide-de-camp and counsellor.

Together we formed the plan of attack. It was resolved that one half our company, under de Villiers himself, should fall upon the isolated party in the lane and cut them to pieces. That left us but two hundred men with whom to engage the remaining three hundred and fifty of the New Englanders, — a daring venture, but I undertook to lead it. I undertook by no means to defeat them, however. I knew the fine mettle of these vinegar-faced New Englanders, but I swore (and kept my oath) that I would occupy them pleasantly till de Villiers, making an end of the other detachment, should come to my aid and clinch the victory.

The plan of attack thus settled, I turned my attention to Philip. Nigh at hand was a cottage where I was known, — where I believed the folk to be very kindly and honest. I told Big Etienne that we would put the child there to sleep, and after the battle take him to his mother at Canard.

"And, my brother," said I, laying my hand on his arm, and looking into his eyes with meaning, "let Xavier stay with him, for he will be afraid among strangers."

"Xavier must fight," replied the tall warrior. But his eyes shifted from mine, and there was indecision in his voice.

"Xavier is but a boy yet, my brother," I insisted. "And this is a night attack. It is no place for an untried boy. No glory, but great peril, for one who has not experience! For my sake bid Xavier stay with the child."

"You are right, brother. He shall stay," said the Indian.

And Xavier was not consulted. He stayed. But his was a face of sore disappointment when we left him with Philip at the cottage, — "to guard with your life, if need be!" said I, in going. And thus gave him a sense of responsibility and peril to cheer his bitter inaction.

It had been snowing all day, but lightly. After nightfall there blew up a fitful wind, now fierce, now breathless. At one moment the air would be thick with drift, and the great blasts would buffet us in the teeth. At another, there would seem to be in all the dim-glimmering world no movement and no breathing but our own.

It was far past midnight when we came upon the hill-slope overlooking Grand Pré village; and the village was asleep. Not a light was visible save in one long row of cottages at the extreme east end, close by the water side. Thither, at our orders, the villagers had quietly withdrawn before midnight. The rash New England men lay sleeping, with apparently no guards set. If there were sentries, then the storm had driven them indoors.

The great gusts swirled and roared past their windows, piling the drift more deeply about their thresholds. If any woke, they turned perchance luxuriously in their beds and listened to the blasts, and praised God that the Acadian peasants builded their houses warm. They had no thought of the ruin that drew near through the drifts and the whirling darkness. I have never heard that one of them was kept awake with strange terrors, or had any prevision, or made special searching of his soul before sleep.

It would seem as if Heaven must have forgotten them for a little. Or perhaps the saints remembered that the English were not a people to take advice kindly, or to change their plans for any sort of warning that might seem to them irregular. But among us French, that night, there was one at least who was granted some prevision.

Just before the two columns separated, Tamin came to me and wrung my hand. He was with de Villiers' detachment. There was a certain awe, a something of farewell, in his manner, and it moved my heart mightily. But I clapped him on the back. "No forebodings, now, my friend," said I; "keep a good heart and your eyes wide open."

"The snow is deep to-night, Monsieur!" said he gravely, as he turned away.

"True," I answered; "but the apple trees are at the other end of the village; and who ever heard that the Black Abbé was a prophet?"

Even as I spoke my heart smote me, and I would have given much to wring the loyal fellow's hand once more. But I feared to add to his depression.

My men all knew their parts before I led them from the camp. Once in the village, only a few whispered orders were necessary. Squad by squad, dim forms like phantoms in the drift, filed off stealthily to their places.

I, with two dozen others, Big Etienne at my elbow, took post about the centre of the village, where three large houses, joined together, seemed to promise a rough bout. Then we waited. Saints, how long we waited, as it seemed! The snow invaded us. But the apple trees were many, and we leaned against them, gnawing our fingers, and protecting our primings with the long flaps of our coats. At last there came a musket-shot from the far-off lane, and straightway thereupon a crashing volley, followed by a dreadful outcry—shouts and screams, and the yelling of the Indians.

Our waiting was done. We sprang forward to dash in the nearest windows, to batter down the nearest doors. Lights gleamed. Then came crashes of musketry from the points where I had placed my several parties, and I knew they had found their posts. The fight once begun, there was little room for generalship in that driven and shrieking dark.

I could see but what was before me. In those three houses there were brave men, that I knew. Springing from sleep in their shirts, they seemed to wake full armed, and were already firing upon us as we tried to force our way in through the windows. The main door of the biggest house we strove to carry with a rush, but that, too, belched lead and fire in our faces, and we came upon a barrier of household stuff just inside. By the light of a musket flash, I saw a huge, sour-faced fellow in his shirt, standing on the barrier, with his gun-stock swung back. I made at him nimbly with my sword. I reached him, and the uplifted weapon fell somewhere harmless in the dark. The next moment I felt a sword point, thrusting blindly, furrow across my temple, tearing as if it were both hot and dull, and at the same instant I was dragged out again into the snow. Three of us, however, as I learned afterwards, stayed on the floor within.

It was Big Etienne who had saved me. I was dizzy for a moment with my wound, the blood throbbing down in a flood; but I ordered all to fall back under the shelter of the apple trees, and keep up a steady firing upon the doors and windows. The order was passed along, and in a few minutes the firing was steady. Then winding my kerchief tightly about my temples, I bade Big Etienne knot it for me, and for the time I thought no more of that sword-scratch.

Though my men were heavily outnumbered, the enemy could not guess how few we were. Moreover, we had the shelter of the trees, and our fire had their windows to converge upon. We held them, therefore, with no great loss, except for those that fell in the first onslaught, which was bloody for both sides. Presently a tongue of flame shot up, and I knew that they had set fire to one of the houses on the lane. The shouting there, and the yelling, died away, but a scattering crackle of musketry continued. Then another building burst into flame. The night grew all one red, wavering glare. As the smoke clouds blew this way and that, the

shadows rose and fell. The squalls of
drift blurred everything; but in the ·lulls
men stood out suddenly as simple targets,
and were shot with great precision. Yet
we had shelter enough, too; for every
house, every barn and shed, cast a block
of thick darkness on its northern side.
Then men began to gather in upon the
centre. Here a squad of my own fellows
— yelling and cheering with triumph, if
they were Indians, quietly exultant if they
were veterans — would come from the
conquest of a cottage. There a knot of
half-clad English, fleeing reluctantly and
firing over their shoulders as they fled,
would arrive, beat at the doors before us,
and be let in hastily under our fire, leaving always some of their number on the
threshold. It was like no other fight I
had ever fought, for the strange confusion
of it; or perhaps my wound confused me
yet a little. At length a louder yelling,
a sharper firing, a wilder and mightier
clamour, arose in the direction of the lane.
Our own firing slackened. All eyes turned
to watch a little band which, fighting furi-

ously, was forcing its way hither through a swarm of assailants. "The vinegar-faces can fight!" I cried, "but we must stop them. Come on, lads!" And with a score at my back I rushed to meet the new-comers. Rushed, did I say? But I should have said struggled and floundered. For, the moment we were clear of the trampled area, and found ourselves in the open fields, the snow went nearly to our middles. Yet we met the gallant little band, which having shaken off its assailants, now fell upon us with a welcome of most earnest curses. Men speak of the bloody ferocity of a duel in a dark room. It is nothing to the blind, blundering, reckless, snarling rage of that struggle in the deep snow, and under that swimming delusive light. Having emptied my musket and my pistols, I threw them all away, and fell to playing nimbly with my sword. Big Etienne I saw close beside me, swinging his musket by the barrel. Suddenly its deadly sweep missed its object. The tall warrior fell headforemost, carried off his uneasy balance by the force of the blow. Ere he could flounder up again a foeman was upon him with uplifted sword. But with a mighty lunge, hurling myself forward from the drift that held my feet, I reached the man's neck with my own point, and fell at his feet. He came down in a heap on top of me. His knee, as I suppose it was, struck me violently on the head. Perhaps I was already weakened by that cut upon the temple. The noise all died suddenly away. I remember thinking how warm the snow felt against my face. And the rest of the fight was no concern of mine.

Chapter XXII

The Black Abbé Strikes in the Dark

I WAS awakened to consciousness by some one gently lifting me. I struggled at once to my feet, leaning upon him. It was Big Etienne.

"You much hurt?" he queried, in great concern.

"Why, no!" said I, presently. "Head feels sore. I think I'll be all right in a minute."

It was in the red and saffron of dawn. The snow had stopped falling. The muskets had stopped clattering. The battle was apparently at an end. All around lay bodies, or rather parts of bodies; for they were more or less hidden in the snow. Close by me just a pair of knees was visible, thrust up through a drift into which the man had plunged in falling.

The snow was all mottled with blood and powder, a very hideous colour to look upon. I stood erect and stretched myself.

"Why, brother," I exclaimed, in great relief, "I am as good as new. Where is the commander?"

Big Etienne pointed in silence to the street before the three houses. There I saw our men drawn up in menacing array. In and behind the houses were crowded the dark masses of the New Englanders, punctuated here and there with the scarlet of an officer's coat.

De Villiers greeted me as one recovered from the grave. I asked eagerly how he had sped, and how the matter now rested.

"Success, everywhere success, Briart!" he answered, with a sort of controlled elation. "You held these fellows, while we wiped out those yonder. But it was a cruel and bloody affair, and I would the times, and the straits of New France, required not such killing in the dark. But they set fire to a house and barn that they might fight in the light, and so a band of them escaped us and cut their way through here, — what was left of them, at least, after they got done with you!   And now their remnant is hemmed in yonder."

" We've got them, then," said I.

" Surely," he answered.   " But it will cost our best blood to end it.   They have fought like heroes, though they kept guard like fools.   And they will battle it out, I think, while a man of them stands."

" Yes, 'tis the breed of them!" said I, looking across with admiration at the silent and dangerous ranks.   " But they have done all that brave men could do.   They will accept honourable terms, I think; and such we may offer them without any touch of discredit.   What do you say?"

This was, indeed what de Villiers had in his heart.   He withdrew his troops some little distance, that negotiations might be the less embarrassed; and I myself, feeling a fresh dizziness, retired to a cottage where I might have my

wound properly tended. But barely had
I got the bandage loosened, — a black-
eyed Acadian maid standing by, with
face of deep commiseration and holding
a basin of hot water for me, — when there
broke out a sudden firing. I clapped the
bloody bandage to my head, and ran
forth; but I saw there was no need of
me. The English had sallied with a fierce
heat, hoping to retrieve their fortunes.
But the deep snow was like an army to
shut them in. Before they could come at
us they were exhausted, and our muskets
dropped them swiftly in the drifts. Sul-
lenly they fell back again upon their
houses. I turned to my basin and my
bandaging.

"That settles that!" said I to the
damsel.

"Settles what, Monsieur?" she asked.
But as she spoke I saw a look of sudden
concern cross her face, a faintness came
over me, and I lay down, feeling her arm
support me as I sank.

Sleep is the best of medicines for me.
I woke late in the afternoon to find my

head neatly bandaged, and the dizziness all gone. Men came and went softly. I found that de Villiers was lying in the same house, having got a serious wound just after I left him. La Corne, a brave Canadian, was in command. The English had capitulated toward noon, and had pledged themselves to depart for Annapolis within forty-eight hours, not to bear arms again in Acadie within six months. We had redeemed at Grand Pré our late failure at Annapolis.

My first act was to send a runner, on snow-shoes, to Canard, with a scrawled note to Mizpah. Explaining nothing, I merely begged that she and Prudence, with Marc and Father Fafard, should meet me at the Forge about noon of the following day. In the case of Marc not being yet strong enough to journey so far, I prayed Mizpah herself, in any event, to come without fail. My next was to send a messenger for Xavier and Philip. My heart had fallen to aching curiously for the child, — insomuch that I marvelled at it, till at length I set it

down as a mere whimsical counterfeit of
my longing for his mother.

Being now refreshed and altogether
myself again, I went to visit the lane
wherein the fight had opened. The very
first house, whose shattered door and
windows, blood-smeared threshold, and
dripping window-sills, showed that the
fight had there raged long and madly,
had one great apple tree beside its garden gate. A chill of foreboding smote
me as I marked it. I approached with a
curious and painful expectancy, the words
of the Black Abbé ringing again in my
ears. At the foot of the apple tree the
snow was drifted deep. It half covered a
pitifully huddled body.

I lifted the body. It was Tamin.

He had been shot through the lungs,
and his blood, melting the snow, had
gathered in a crimson pool beneath him.
Here was one grim prophecy fulfilled.
Carrying him into the house, I laid him
gently on a bed. Then I turned away
with a very sorrowful heart; for there was
much to do, and the dead are not urgent.

Even as I turned, my heart jumped with a new and sickening dread. Xavier stood before me — Xavier, with wild eyes, and face darkly clotted with blood. The next instant he threw himself at my feet.

"The child!" he muttered, covering his face. "They have carried him away. They have carried Philip away!"

"What do you mean?" I cried, in a voice which my fear made harsh, while at the same time I dragged him to his feet. "Who have carried him away? Who?"

But I knew the answer ere he could speak it, — I knew my enemy had seized the chances of the battle and the night.

"The Black Abbé," wailed the lad, in a voice of poignant sorrow. "He came in the night, with two Chepody Acadians dressed up like Indians, and seized me asleep, and bound me."

"But Philip!" I cried. "Where have they taken him?" And even as I spoke I was planning swiftly.

"The Abbé started westward with him," answered Xavier. "From what

I heard say, he would go to Pereau; but which way after, I could not find out."

" Come ! " I ordered roughly, " we must follow them ! "   But as I spoke I saw the lad totter.   I caught him by the arm and held him up, perceiving now for the first time how he was both wounded and utterly spent.

" Let us go first to your father," I said more gently, leading him, and putting what curb I could upon the fierceness of my haste.

" How did you get here ? " I asked him presently.

A gleam came into the lad's faint eyes.

" The Chepody men stayed till morning," said he, " and then set out on the road toward Piziquid, taking me with them.   They thought I was nothing but a boy.   As we went, I got my hands loose, so, — and waited.   At noon one man went into a house, — and — *so !* — I was free, and had the other dog by the throat.   He make no noise; but he fight hard, and hurt me.   I got away, and left him in the snow, and ran back all the way to tell you the Black Abbé — "

But here the poor lad's voice failed, and he hung upon me with all his weight. He had fainted, indeed; and now that I thought of his wound, his hunger, his grief, and his prodigious exertions, I wondered not at his swooning. Picking him up in my arms, I carried him to the cottage where the kind damsel had so compassionately tended my own bruises.

As I entered the thronged cottage with my burden, men came about me with many questions; but I kept my own counsel, not knowing whom I could trust, or where the Black Abbé might not have his spies posted. Moreover, I was so distracted with anxiety about the child, that I had small patience wherewith to take questioning civilly. Every bed and every settle being occupied with our wounded, I laid Xavier on the floor, with his head upon a blue petticoat which the kind damsel — who came to me as soon as she saw me enter — fetched from a cupboard and rolled up deftly for me. After a careful examination I found no wound upon the lad save two shallow flesh cuts, one across his forehead and one down his chest. I thereupon concluded that exhaustion, together with the loss of blood, had brought him to this pass, and that with a few days' care he would be altogether restored. Having put some brandy between his lips, and seen his eyelids tremble with recovering consciousness, I turned to the maiden and said:—

"Take care of him for me, Chérie. He deserves your best care; and I trust him to your good heart. Give him something to eat now,—soup, hot milk, at first. And I will come back in two days from now, at furthest."

"But Monsieur must rest!"

"No rest for me to-night!" I interrupted, in a low voice, as I straightened myself up. "Do you know where I may find the lad's father, the chief, Big—"

But there was no need for me to finish the question. There, close behind me, stood the tall Indian, looking down at

Xavier, with trouble in his eyes.   He had just entered, in his silent fashion.

"There is no danger!   He is worn out!" I whispered.   "He has done all a brave man could do; but the child is stolen!   Come outside with me."

Big Etienne stooped quickly and laid his hand upon the lad's breast, and then, most gently, upon his lips.   A second later he had followed me out into the deepening twilight.

In few words I told him what had happened, and my purpose of going instantly in pursuit.   Without a word he strode off toward a small cabin about a stone's throw from the cottage which we had just left.

"Where are you going?" I asked, astonished at this abruptness.

"My snow-shoes!" he replied.   "And bread.   I go with you, my brother!"

This, in very truth, was just what I had hoped for.   But, in my haste, I had forgotten the need of eating; and, as for my snow-shoes, usually strapped at my back, they had been left at the outskirts of the village the night before in order that my sword arm might have the freer play. It was no time now to go back for them. I slipped into the cottage, borrowed a pair, and was presently forth again to meet Big Etienne. The Indian, instead of bread, had brought a goodly lump of dried beef. Side by side, and in silence, we set out for the cabin on the Gaspereau where Philip and Xavier had been captured.

We found the place deserted. Either the man of the house had been a tool of La Garne, or he feared that I would hold him responsible. Which it was, I know not to this day ; and, at the time, we gave small thought to the question, merely commending the fellow's wisdom in removing himself from our indignation. What engaged our concern was a single snow-shoe track making westward, followed by the trail of a little sledge.

" Yes," said I ; " Xavier is surely right. The Abbé has gone to cross the Habitants and the Canard where they are little, and will then, belike, turn down the valley to Pereau ! "

"Very like!" grunted my companion; and, at a long lope, we started up the trail.

This pace, however, soon told upon me, and brought it into my mind that I had, that day, eaten nothing but a bowl of broth. We halted, therefore, and rested half an hour in the warmth of a dense spruce coppice, and ate abundantly of that very savoury beef. Then, much revived, we set out again. Treading one behind the other, we marched, in silence, through the glimmering dark; for Big Etienne was no talker, while I, for my part, was gnawing my heart with rage, and hope frustrated, and the picture of Mizpah's anguish. We never stayed our pace till we came, at the edge of dawn, to the spot where the trail went over the dwindled upper current of the Habitants.

Here, to our astonishment, the trail turned eastward, following down the course of the river.

I looked at the Indian in wondering consternation. "What can it mean?" I cried. "Can there be any new plot of his hatching at Canard?"

"Maybe!" said Big Etienne.

At thought of further perils threatening Mizpah and Marc, the weariness which had been growing upon me vanished, and I sprang forward as briskly as if we had but just set out. Even Big Etienne, though he had no such incentive as mine, seemed to win new vigour with the contemplation of this new coil of the enemy's. If, indeed, he appeared somewhat fresher than I throughout the latter half of this hard march, it is but justice to myself to say that he bore no wound from the late battle.

At last, when it was well past ten of the morning, the trail led us out upon the main Canard track, and turned toward the settlement.

"Yes," said I, with bitter conviction; "he has gone to Canard. He would never go there had he not some deep scheme of mischief afoot. God grant we be in time!"

In less than half an hour we came within sight of the Forge in the Forest. To my astonishment, the smoke was pouring in furious volume from the forge chimney.

"What can Babin be about? Or can Mizpah and Marc be there already?" I wondered aloud; but got no answer from my companion. A moment later, a turn of the track brought us to a post of vantage whence we could see straight into the forge. The sight which met our eyes brought us to an instant stop from sheer amazement.

Chapter XXIII

The Rendezvous at the Forge

BESIDE the forge-fire stood Grûl. On his left arm was perched Philip, half wrapped in the black-and-yellow cloak, and playing with Grûl's white wand. At the back of the forge, fettered to the wall, and with his hands bound behind him, stood the black form of our adversary. Grûl was heaving upon the bellows, and in the fierce white glow of the coal stuck a number of irons heating. These he turned and twisted with fantastic energy, now and then drawing one forth and brandishing it with a kind of mad glee, so as best to show the intensity of its colour; and whenever he did so little Philip shouted with delight.

The joy that surged through my breast as I took in all this astonishing turn of affairs, was something which I have no words to tell of.

" Mary, Mother of Heaven, be praised for this!" I cried fervently.

" What will he do with irons?" queried Big Etienne, with a curiously startled note in his voice.

Indeed, what now followed was sufficiently startling. Grûl had caught sight of us. Immediately he set the child down, heaved twice or thrice mightily upon the bellows, and then drew from the fire two white-hot rods of iron. With these, one in each hand, he approached the Black Abbé, treading swiftly and sinuously like a panther. I darted forward, chilled with sudden horror. A short scream of mortal fear came from the wretched captive's lips.

" Stop! stop!" I shouted, as those terrible brands went circling hither and thither about the cringing form. The next instant, and ere I could reach the scene to interfere, the Abbé gave a huge bound, reached the door, and plunged out into the snow, pursued by a peal of wild laughter from Grûl's lips. This most whimsical of madmen had befooled his captive, in much the same fashion as once before on the cliff beside the des Saumons. He had used the deadly iron merely to free him from his bonds, and again held in reserve his full vengeance.

Fetching a huge breath of relief, I joined in Grûl's mocking laughter; while Big Etienne gave a grunt of manifest dissatisfaction. As for the Black Abbé, though the sweat of his terror stood in beads upon his forehead, he recovered his composure marvellously. Having run some dozen paces he stopped, turned, and gazed steadily upon Grûl for perhaps the space of a full minute. Then, sweeping a scornful glance across the child, the Indian, and myself, he half opened his lips to speak. But if he judged himself not then best ready to speak with dignity,— let no one marvel at that. He changed his purpose, folded his arms across his breast, and strode off slowly and in silence along the track toward Grand Pré.

I thought his shadow, as it fell long

and sinister across the snow, lay blacker than was the common wont of shadows.

Big Etienne was already within, and Philip in his arms. As I entered the forge door Grûl cried solemnly, as if to extenuate his act in freeing the prisoner : —

"His cup is not yet full."

Seizing both his hands in mine, I tried with stammering lips to thank him; but, something to my chagrin, he cut me short most ungraciously. Snatching his hands away, he stepped outside the door, and raised his thrilling, bell-like chant : —

"Woe, woe to Acadie the Fair, for the day of her desolation cometh."

Beyond all words though my gratitude was, I could not refrain from shrugging my shoulders at this fantastic mummery, as I turned to embrace little Philip. My heart was rioting with joy and hope, and I could not trouble my wits with these mad whimsies of Grûl's. When he had quit prophesying and come again within the forge, I tried to draw from him some account of how he had so achieved the child's rescue and the Black Abbé's utter discomfiture. But he wandered from the matter, whether wilfully or not I could by no means decide; and presently, catching a ghost of a smile on the face of Big Etienne, I gave up and rested thankful for what I had got. As for Philip, he was amiably gracious to both Big Etienne and myself, but it was manifest that all his little heart had gone out to Grûl; and the two were presently playing together in a corner of the forge, at some game which none but themselves could understand.

It wanted yet an hour of noon, when, as I stood in the door consuming my heart with impatience, yet unwilling to go and meet Mizpah and so mar the climax which I had plotted for, I caught sight of two figures approaching. I needed not eyes to tell me one was Mizpah, for the blood shook in all my veins at sight of her. The other was Father Fafard.

" Marc," said I to myself, " is not yet

strong enough to venture so far; and the maid Prudence has stayed with him.   But Mizpah is here — Mizpah is here!"

With eyes of delight I dwelt upon her tall, slim form, in its gown of blue woollen cloth which set off so rarely the red-gold enchantment of her hair.   But when she was come near enough for me to mark the eager welcome in her eyes and on her lips, I waved at her, clumsily enough, and turned within to catch at a little self-possession.   Not having my snow-shoes on, I could not be expected to go and meet her; and that waiting in the doorway was too much for me to endure.

"Keep Philip behind the chimney, out of sight," I whispered eagerly to Grûl; and somewhat to my wonder he obeyed.

On the next instant Mizpah stood in the door, smiling upon me, her face all aglow with expectation and greeting; and I found myself clasping both of her white hands.   But my tongue refused to speak, — deeming, perchance, that my eyes were usurping its office.

Finding at length a word of welcome

for the good priest, I wrung his hand fervently, then turned again to Mizpah.

But my first speech was stupid, — so stupid that I wished most heartily that I had held my tongue.

"Comrade," said I, "this is a glad day for me."

Her face fell, and her eyes reproached me.

"Because you have defeated and slain my people?" she asked.

My face grew hot for the flat ineptitude of my words.

"No! no! Not for that!" I cried passionately, "but for *this!*"

And I turned to snatch Philip from his corner behind the chimney.

But Grûl was too quick for me. He could play no second part at any time, he. Evading my hands, he slipped past me, and himself placed the child in Mizpah's arms.

I cursed inwardly at his abruptness, though in truth he had done just what I was intending to do myself. As Mizpah, with a gasping cry, crushed the little one to her bosom, she went white as a ghost and tottered against the anvil. I sprang to support her, but withheld my arm ere it touched her waist, for even on the instant she had recovered herself. With wordless mother-cries she kissed Philip's lips and hair, and buried her face in his neck, he the while clinging to her as if never again for a moment could he let her go.

Presently, while I waited in great hunger for a word, she turned to Big Etienne and Grûl.

"My friends!" she cried, in a shaken voice which faithfully uttered her heart, "my true and loyal friends!" Whereupon she wrung their hands, and wrung them, and would have spoken further but that her voice failed her.

Then, after a moment or two, she turned to me, — yet not wholly.

The paleness had by this well vanished, and her eyes, those great sea-coloured eyes, which she would not lift to mine, were running over with tears. Philip took one sturdy little arm from her neck,

and stretched out his hand to me ; but I
ignored the invitation.

"And what — what have you got for
me, Mizpah?" I asked, in a very low
voice, indeed — a voice perhaps not just
as steady as that of a noted bush-fighter
is supposed to be at a crisis.

The flush grew, deepening down along
the clear whiteness of her neck, and she
half put out one hand to me.

"Do you want thanks?" she asked
softly.

"You *know* what I want, — what I
have wanted above all else in life from
the moment my eyes fell upon you!"
I cried with a great passion, grown suddenly forgetful of Grûl and Big Etienne,
who doubtless found my emotion more
or less interesting.

For a second or two Mizpah made no
answer.   Then she lifted her face, gave
me one swift look straight in the eyes,
— a look that told me all I longed to
know, — and suddenly, with a little laugh
that was mostly a sob, put Philip into my
arms.

"AND SUDDENLY . . . PUT PHILIP INTO MY ARMS"

"There!" she whispered, dropping her eyes.

And by some means it so came about that, as I took the child, my arms held Mizpah also.

THE END

FAMOUS COPYRIGHT BOOKS IN POPULAR PRICED EDITIONS

Re-issues of the great literary successes of the time. Library size. Printed on excellent paper—most of them with illustrations of marked beauty—and handsomely bound in cloth. Price, 75 cents a volume, postpaid.

LAVENDER AND OLD LACE. By Myrtle Reed.

A charming story of a quaint corner of New England where bygone romance finds a modern parallel. One of the prettiest, sweetest, and quaintest of old-fashioned love stories * * * A rare book, exquisite in spirit and conception, full of delicate fancy, of tenderness, of delightful humor and spontaneity. A dainty volume, especially suitable for a gift.

DOCTOR LUKE OF THE LABRADOR. By Norman Duncan. With a frontispiece and inlay cover.

How the doctor came to the bleak Labrador coast and there in saving life made expiation. In dignity, simplicity, humor, in sympathetic etching of a sturdy fisher people, and above all in the echoes of the sea, *Doctor Luke* is worthy of great praise. Character, humor, poignant pathos, and the sad grotesque conjunctions of old and new civilizations are expressed through the medium of a style that has distinction and strikes a note of rare personality.

THE DAY'S WORK. By Rudyard Kipling. Illustrated.

The *London Morning Post* says: "It would be hard to find better reading * * * the book is so varied, so full of color and life from end to end, that few who read the first two or three stories will lay it down till they have read the last—and the last is a veritable gem * * * contains some of the best of his highly vivid work * * * Kipling is a born story-teller and a man of humor into the bargain.

ELEANOR LEE. By Margaret E. Sangster. With a frontispiece.

A story of married life, and attractive picture of wedded bliss * * an entertaining story or a man's redemption through a woman's love * * * no one who knows anything of marriage or parenthood can read this story with eyes that are always dry * * * goes straight to the heart of every one who knows the meaning of "love" and "home."

THE COLONEL OF THE RED HUZZARS. By John Reed Scott. Illustrated by Clarence F. Underwood.

"Full of absorbing charm, sustained interest, and a wealth of thrilling and romantic situations. "So naively fresh in its handling, so plausible through its naturalness, that it comes like a mountain breeze across the far-spreading desert of similar romances."—*Gazette-Times, Pittsburg.* "A slap-dashing day romance."—*New York Sun.*

GROSSET & DUNLAP, - NEW YORK

FAMOUS COPYRIGHT BOOKS
IN POPULAR PRICED EDITIONS

Re-issues of the great literary successes of the time, library size, printed on excellent paper—most of them finely illustrated. Full and handsomely bound in cloth. Price, 75 cents a volume, postpaid.

THE CATTLE BARON'S DAUGHTER. A Novel. By Harold Bindloss. With illustrations by David Ericson.

A story of the fight for the cattle-ranges of the West. Intense interest is aroused by its pictures of life in the cattle country at that critical moment of transition when the great tracts of land used for grazing were taken up by the incoming homesteaders, with the inevitable result of fierce contest, of passionate emotion on both sides, and of final triumph of the inevitable tendency of the times.

WINSTON OF THE PRAIRIE. With illustrations in color by W. Herbert Dunton.

A man of upright character, young and clean, but badly worsted in the battle of life, consents as a desperate resort to impersonate for a period a man of his own age—scoundrelly in character but of an aristocratic and moneyed family. The better man finds himself barred from resuming his old name. How, coming into the other man's possessions, he wins the respect of all men, and the love of a fastidious, delicately nurtured girl, is the thread upon which the story hangs. It is one of the best novels of the West that has appeared for years.

THAT MAINWARING AFFAIR. By A. Maynard Barbour. With illustrations by E. Plaisted Abbott.

A novel with a most intricate and carefully unraveled plot. A naturally probable and excellently developed story and the reader will follow the fortunes of each character with unabating interest * * * the interest is keen at the close of the first chapter and increases to the end.

AT THE TIME APPOINTED. With a frontispiece in colors by J. H. Marchand.

The fortunes of a young mining engineer who through an accident loses his memory and identity. In his new character and under his new name, the hero lives a new life of struggle and adventure. The volume will be found highly entertaining by those who appreciate a thoroughly good story.

GROSSET & DUNLAP, Publishers,   -   -   New York

www.ingramcontent.com/pod-product-compliance
Lightning Source LLC
Chambersburg PA
CBHW031151120726
47905CB00006B/1901